She Professed Herself Pupil of the Wise Man

NOVEL 1

WRITTEN BY

Ryusen Hirotsugu

ILLUSTRATED BY

fuzichoco

Airship

Seven Seas Entertainment

TABLE OF CONTENTS

Kenja no deshi wo nanoru kenja
©Ryusen Hirotsugu (Story) ©fuzichoco (Illustrations)
This edition originally published in Japan in 2014 by
MICRO MAGAZINE, INC., Tokyo.
English translation rights arranged with
MICRO MAGAZINE, INC., Tokyo.

Seven Seas press and purchase enquiries can be sent to
Marketing Manager Lianne Sentar at press@gomanga.com.
Information regarding the distribution and purchase of
digital editions is available from Digital Manager CK Russell
at digital@gomanga.com.

Seven Seas and the Seven Seas logo are trademarks of
Seven Seas Entertainment. All rights reserved.

Follow Seven Seas Entertainment online at
sevenseasentertainment.com.

TRANSLATION: Wesley O'Donnell
ADAPTATION: Adam Lee
COVER DESIGN: Nicky Lim
LOGO DESIGN: George Panella
INTERIOR LAYOUT & DESIGN: Clay Gardner
PROOFREADER: Meg van Huygen, Teiko
LIGHT NOVEL EDITOR: Rebecca Scoble
PREPRESS TECHNICIAN: Rhiannon Rasmussen-Silverstein
PRODUCTION MANAGER: Lissa Pattillo
MANAGING EDITOR: Julie Davis
ASSOCIATE PUBLISHER: Adam Arnold
PUBLISHER: Jason DeAngelis

ISBN: 978-1-64827-423-7
Printed in Canada
First Printing: September 2021
10 9 8 7 6 5 4 3 2 1

PROLOGUE

A T THE DAWN of the twenty-second century, society found itself transformed by the emergence of practical VR technology.

Students no longer attended classes in person. They connected to their schools from dedicated terminals in their homes without the hassles of commuting and early morning wake-ups. School districts benefited as well, channeling precious funding into quality education programs instead of facility maintenance and upkeep.

The corporate world also adopted VR, allowing companies to interact with clients and customers remotely. The reliance on automation and computer systems streamlined business and eliminated legacy paperwork filing systems. Like the education system, it was cheaper to do business in the virtual world on a rented server than it was to maintain brick-and-mortar offices and storefronts.

As the paradigm shift occurred, the rate of technological advance accelerated. It became commonplace for young adults to receive the latest VR setup as a graduation gift. While the intent of these gifts might have been to allow them to enter the workforce smoothly, the reality was that few sectors of the economy reaped the benefits of this change like the video game industry.

Sakamori Kagami was a young man who worked for a small company using his VR kit. He had no commute, he worked very little overtime, and he still lived at home and enjoyed his mother's cooking. He had no complaints.

And Sakamori Kagami was a gamer.

One night, Kagami was perplexed by a late-night commercial. It was a silent static image, just a VR access code with the words *Ark Earth Online* printed below. Hardly anyone noticed it at that time of night, but he managed to grab a screenshot before it disappeared.

His curiosity was piqued, and he logged into his VR kit to enter the code. A white virtual void greeted him with the title of the game floating before him. Two buttons hovered just below the title. His choices were:

Begin Open Beta
Download

He liked the game's unpretentious attitude, so he clicked *Download*. After agreeing to a boilerplate EULA, the status bar began to fill, and he passed the time by wondering what kind of game this would be. Something about it called to him. Deep down, he knew that it would be life-changing.

Fifteen minutes later, a home screen with a photorealistic background of a fantasy-world landscape appeared. Kagami clicked on *Begin Open Beta* and stepped into the world of *Ark Earth Online*.

For such a low-key launch, the game caught on like wildfire, and soon the servers had populations that rivaled those of big-studio releases. This was a testament to the game's quality, considering the total lack of advertisement. No full-page spreads were purchased in any gaming publications, and no banner ads littered websites. It was an underground phenomenon entirely spread by word of mouth.

Adding to the mystery was the total media blackout around those who ran the game. Who was the dev team? What new features were planned? No one knew. There was no official website, and the updates occurred without warning. Players just logged in to find patch notes and enhanced features.

Ark Earth Online's basic premise was nothing new—pretty orthodox medieval/fantasy fare. But what made the game stand out was the overwhelming degree of freedom that players were allowed. The hands-off approach by *AEO*'s developers extended to nearly every aspect of gameplay, and the players adored it.

Most importantly, though: it was bug-free.

Kagami spent hours just crafting and maintaining his character's appearance each week. He had white hair and a long beard, befitting his image as a powerful elder sorcerer. Flowing robes of exotic fabric clothed his distinguished form. Even his name was chosen with the utmost care and attention. He drew his inspiration from the great magicians of two literary classics: the headmaster of a certain school of wizardry and the gray eminence who organized a quest to destroy an evil ring. Everyone at work knew him as Sakamori Kagami, but to the players of *Ark Earth Online* he was known as the Summoner, Danblf Gandador.

From the very beginning, Kagami had chosen the mage's path. The problem was that *AEO* was an incredibly free-form game; there were no tutorials that detailed how to use or learn magic, and the learning curve was brutal. No matter how many enemies he killed, no matter where he looked, he couldn't find a way to learn new spells.

Finally, someone on the message boards made a brief post that pointed him in the right direction. A mage could learn a summoning spell either by forming contracts with the spirits of slain enemies or by completing a chain of quests that started with burning a piece of inscribed paper using the beginner's Flame technique. With those humble pearls of wisdom, Danblf would forge himself into the game's preeminent summoner.

The game delighted in providing players with a great sense of accomplishment through hard work. At times, it was fraught with hardships, but many opportunities awaited those who stuck

it out. Through work and diplomacy, a player could become a king, develop a city, muster an army, and invade other countries.

Possibilities were limitless, even for those without the ambition to rule. One player founded a dojo to teach a system of martial arts developed wholly within the game. Spies and merchants, adventurers and cultists, assassins and farmers—everyone was fully engrossed in the idea of being the author of their own story.

Players speculated that anything possible in real life could also be done in the game. They began to make names for themselves as craftsmen and artisans. Certain blacksmiths became so well known for the quality of their work that a single sword from their forge would sell for millions of ducats, the in-game currency. Others mastered carpentry and masonry, developing architecture and building techniques that allowed for the construction of mighty castles.

There was even a player who became obsessed with digging holes. They stumbled across a hot spring and turned it into a lucrative in-game spa and resort.

The only limit to what a player could do was the time they were willing to invest discovering and honing their skills. Those skills were cataloged by yet another player, who conducted a census of the player base. His encyclopedia of techniques became an instant in-game success, earning him a small fortune.

Danblf had even developed an entirely new class. Through a regimen of standing under waterfalls and hanging upside down from trees, he unlocked the Sage profession and pioneered the practice of Dual Classing. It was a breakthrough born of necessity—summoners and other magic users were woefully unequipped to deal with hand-to-hand combat, and that made their early progression very difficult. By Dual Classing as a Sage, Danblf was able to use mystical punches and kicks to handle opponents when they got too close for comfort.

As long as he was playing *Ark Earth Online,* Kagami was in his element. Four years after he read a couple of hints on a message board, Danblf Gandador rose to become one of the leaders of his country—one of the Nine Wise Men.

Leadership came with responsibility.

One evening, Danblf was tasked with wiping out a group of monsters that had appeared near the border of his country. The Wise Men took turns handling these occasional outbreaks, and it was his turn to do the chores.

Leaving his wizard's tower, Danblf began meandering his way to the border when he heard a tone announcing an incoming message from the real world. It was suppertime, and the high-pitched voice of his younger sister called him downstairs to the dinner table. With a sigh, he logged out and removed his headset before joining his family.

Upon his return, he found an email waiting in his inbox. It was a reminder that he still had a balance of 500 yen in the game's cash store that was set to expire the following day.

Like most other games, *AEO* seemed to make most of its

money though a premium store where players traded real-world cash for a variety of in-game goods and services. From cosmetic enhancements to indispensable utility items, nearly every player in the game used the cash store sooner or later.

The problem with the cash store was that a player could only deposit money into their accounts in 1,000-yen increments. It usually worked out because most items were sold in 1,000-yen increments. For instance, a Floating Island sold for 2,000 yen. It was a flying piece of land, roughly twenty-five meters on a side. It could be decorated however the player saw fit, and many players used it as a sort of vehicle to cross over impassable terrain with ease. Players could then buy buildings or terrain features for their island, which sold for 1,000 or 2,000 yen each.

But not *all* items sold in exact multiples of a thousand yen. Somewhere along the line, Kagami had purchased an oddly priced item, leaving him with a dangling balance that would expire if unused.

He had three options. He could add more money to the account and buy something with a nice round price, but that would just kick the can down the road and leave him another 500-yen balance. He could let it expire and write it off as the cost of playing the game. But as much as he loved *AEO*, he didn't feel like giving them money for nothing. The only remaining option was to spend some time finding an item that cost exactly 500 yen.

"Well, that's how they get you," Kagami muttered, looking over his choices.

There was only one—the Vanity Case.

While the basic character creation system gave a player a thousand ways to modify their character's look, the Vanity Case gave *ten* thousand cosmetic options for a measly 500 yen. It was common for most new players to simply choose a default avatar, then spend an entire day tweaking and sculpting their ideal hero with a Vanity Case.

That was how Kagami made Danblf, and it was why there was 500 yen left over in his account to begin with. He sighed, clicked on the item, and watched his balance drop to zero.

Manipulating his armband terminal, he opened the item menu. Inside was a small lacquered box containing the Vanity Case. Four years ago, he'd been so focused on making the ideal distinguished wizard that he couldn't remember any of the other options offered by the creation system.

He was curious. Despite the pressing matter of monster hunting, he couldn't help but open the character editing menu.

In addition to the buttons and sliders, there was a drop-down menu with a number of presets categorized by the attitude they conveyed—*Lively, Stoic, Cheerful, Mysterious*, and so on. As Kagami looked over the list, it reinforced his belief that he'd nailed it on the first try with Danblf. There was simply no way to improve his current avatar.

But as he gazed contentedly at his masterpiece, an option caught his eye: *Male*.

The avatar's gender stared back at Kagami from the menu, and the imp of the perverse began to whisper in his ear. Sure, he'd perfectly created his ideal male form...but what about the ideal *female* form?

He flipped the toggle and Danblf promptly turned into a woman with all of the summoner's features. It was uncanny and uncomfortable to look at. *AEO* might just be a game, but it was still embarrassing to find himself confronted with the female version of his grizzled wizard. Shaking off the cringe, he began to pick through the interface for other options. He selected *Confident* from the presets to see how that looked. Then he kept going.

A while later he gazed in satisfaction at his creation, and a smile crept over his face. His ideal female form stood before him, posing in a looping routine of emotes to show off his handiwork.

Then he heard his sister's voice call him down to breakfast. Checking the clock, he was shocked to see that it was already 9 a.m. Without realizing, he had worked with the Vanity Case all through the night.

A wave of intense drowsiness overcame Kagami. He fumbled for the *Log Out* button in the main menu before fading out.

The world slipped into darkness.

*H*UH, *MUST HAVE* *fallen asleep before I could log out,* Kagami thought.

He looked up at the sky before rubbing the sleep from his eyes. He wasn't sure how long he'd been asleep, but it couldn't have been that long. His little sister would have barged in to wake him up if he'd been napping for more than a few minutes.

Sitting up with a yawn and a stretch, he found himself deep within a forest. Flowers dotted the landscape, and through the swaying trees, he could see the outline of a mountain range. At the foot of the towering peaks, a series of burnished silver towers glinted in the sunlight.

Kagami gazed out at the scenery with his chin in hand as thoughts slowly formed in his foggy mind.

Firstly, why had he passed out while gaming? It was rare but not unheard of. When players fell asleep, the game registered them as AFK and their avatars stopped moving. But under normal circumstances, the game would force sleeping players to log off automatically after a few minutes of inactivity. He'd never heard of anyone waking up inside the game.

And yet, here he was—wide awake and looking at the Linked Silver Towers, home of the Nine Wise Men. He was unmistakably in *AEO*. It might have been a bug, but that would make it the first one that he'd ever encountered.

Another concern that was much more pressing: he could *smell*! The unmistakably natural aroma of a forest's growth and decay tickled his nose on the passing breeze. His VR system could replicate touch and tactile sensations, but taste and smell were still beyond its technical limits as far as he knew. He breathed in through his nose again and marveled at the new, unexplainable sensation.

This called for an additional test. He tore up some nearby grass and gave it a chew. It filled his mouth with the bitter, astringent flavor of grass, and he quickly spat it out before wiping his lips with the back of his hand. The awful taste made him salivate, and even the consistency of the drool was painstakingly reproduced.

Wonder and surprise aside, he couldn't understand how herbivores could stomach such food. He dropped down to take a closer look at the foliage when the high-pitched squeal of metal grinding against metal echoed through the trees. The roar of battle filled the forest and the earth trembled beneath his feet.

This was the *AEO* Danblf recognized!

At least this was easy enough to make sense of. He'd come to the border to subdue a pack of monsters, but someone else had been unlucky enough to run across them first. Or maybe another Wise Man had been assigned to finish the task he had failed to complete last night.

"Ho ho! Not likely," he chuckled to himself as he ran toward the noise.

The woods gave way to a grassy plain where he saw a knight proudly flying a familiar coat of arms. The armored warrior raised his sword and cut down a small green creature wielding a knife. Two or three more goblins bum-rushed the knight as their compatriot fell.

The battlefield was a riot of silver and green. The Magic-Clad Knights charged forth in their gleaming armor with battle cries on their tongues. They were the elite forces of the Kingdom of Alcait, and they descended like an armored wave against the opposing horde of goblins.

Based on the scene before him, Danblf realized he might have slept for longer than he thought. The knights would only be dispatched if he'd taken too much time. It wouldn't do to show up late to a fight and not pull his weight, so he prepared to cast a spell.

[Evocation: Dark Knight]

A dark portal opened above the grass and a large armored form rose from it. The knight was fully encased in chill-inducing jet-black armor, and ominous dark flames flickered about its body. It had no face, just two glowing red lights where eyes should have been. The Dark Knight had arrived.

The monsters stopped in their tracks and shrieked threateningly at Danblf's minion. That was *unnerving*—they shouldn't be programmed to do that. Goblins were cannon fodder. Perhaps they could be described as daring, or at least oblivious to impending danger. They always charged headlong into fights regardless of the odds. But these goblins chittered away in what could only be described as fear.

No matter. There was a time for pondering game mechanics, and a time for action. Danblf gave the Dark Knight the order to attack.

The battle became a massacre. His minion's gigantic sword cut through the air like an arc of lightning. Each violent swing rendered a handful of goblins into bloody chunks and scattered their death cries to the wind. In seconds, the war whoops of the nearby monsters became desperate shrieks. Though they tried to flee or surrender, the Dark Knight's wrath was merciless.

After purging the creatures in its immediate vicinity, the Dark Knight moved to intercept another group of larger goblins wearing bulky armor. Against most assaults, the armor would have been quite resilient—but when the Dark Knight fell upon the pack, their shrieks of terror blended with the shrieks of the summoned knight's sword cutting through the thick metal of their armor. Other goblins had crowded around their larger brethren in hopes of finding safety in numbers, but the Dark Knight cleaved through armored and unarmored monster alike. Their morale broken, the mob began to break ranks and run from the Dark Knight's insatiable bloodlust.

In just a few moments, the entire goblin horde had been routed. A few moments more left them lying dead on the battlefield, the earth stained black with their blood.

It was over. Of the two colors that had once decorated the field, the green was broken and the silver regrouped into formation. The men stood tall but were wary of the Dark Knight.

Must have been nearly a hundred of the little buggers, thought Danblf. He glanced over the bodies to confirm the job was done and dismissed the Dark Knight from the battlefield.

With that chore taken care of, it was back to puzzling over the odd evidence he'd encountered in the past few minutes: the smells, the tastes, the unfamiliar reactions of the goblins. Only one possibility made sense.

There had been an unannounced patch last night.

It was hard to believe that the sense of smell and taste in VR could be reproduced at such an intense level. He was truly experiencing the game world with all five senses. As far as he knew, no other company had developed anything this revolutionary. It was kind of strange that they'd debut a breakthrough technology in a video game, but there was no other possible explanation.

Well, props to the dev team, Danblf decided. *The update was probably why my system didn't shut down when I passed out.*

With that mystery solved, he noticed the sound of clanking armor drawing closer and turned to see a knight bearing a shield engraved with the symbol of the great tree and moon—the coat of arms for the Kingdom of Alcait. Danblf knew that that shield would turn away swords, spells, and dragon fire alike. The elite

knight's mirror-like armor reflected and blended in with his surroundings, and his red cloak marked him as the captain among
his men.

The knight raised a hand to halt his illustrious unit from a
respectful distance away before stepping forward alone. His
swept-back gray hair was flecked with white, and a slanted scar
was carved across his chiseled face like a badge of honor. He was
elegant and handsome—although not at Danblf's level—but his
face was unfamiliar.

Odd. The Wise Man thought he knew all the elite-level cap-
tains in Alcait.

"Pardon me, miss," the captain said. "That knight in the black
armor—I assume that was a summoning technique. Was it yours?
We weren't sure if it was reinforcements or not."

Danblf looked for the person the knight had addressed, but
he found no one else on the battlefield. Was this some sort of
joke? Or an insult? As he glanced around, he saw one of the goblin corpses roll to the side before an unknown creature emerged
from underneath and fled into the forest.

"Hrmmm, so there are still...survi...vors?"

The moment he spoke, he knew two uncomfortable things
were true. The first was that whatever had escaped wasn't a goblin.

"What the hell?!"

The second was that he was speaking in a high, lilting voice.

Danblf stared at the knight, dumbfounded. His image was reflected in the mirror-shined armor of the knight captain standing
before him. He moved his right hand, and the reflection moved

its left. A woman stared back at him and widened her eyes. He was speechless.

He recognized her—silver hair hanging down to her waist, quick-witted blue eyes, cheeks with just a hint of blush, a small nose, and cherubic features. She was wearing Danblf's gear, but the proportions were all wrong.

She was Kagami's ideal female warrior that he'd created with the Vanity Case.

She Professed Herself Pupil of the Wise Man

WHAT THE HELL?! Danblf racked his brain trying to remember what he had done before he passed out.

Meanwhile, the knight captain looked on in bewilderment at the totally spaced-out woman before him. While he waited for her to come back to reality, a few of his subordinates approached with a report about the escaped monster. It was wounded but nimble and had escaped before they could finish it off.

As the captain ordered his men to split into teams and continue pursuit, the woman stared at her reflection in disbelief. Sure enough, the figure staring back was the female avatar that Kagami had created the night before. But *why?* He made the character, sure, but he never actually clicked to confirm the changes. Right?

Slowly, a few details arose from the depths of his memory. He had canceled and logged out... But that was where the memories ended.

Maybe I didn't log out. Did I fall asleep before that? It might have happened before I could hit cancel. Everything after my sister called me for breakfast is a blur.

As he panicked, a thought occurred to him. Using his bracelet terminal to operate the system menu, Danblf navigated to the status screen, which displayed information about his character.

Name: *Danblf Gandador*. That checked out.

Class: *Summoner*. Nothing wrong so far.

His home country and base location were listed correctly as well. His magical power stats were still outstanding, and his physical attributes were in line with most mages. The modifiers his special gear provided to offset lackluster stats also seemed correct.

Everything was exactly like he remembered. He hadn't logged in with the wrong character. Danblf hadn't been deleted. These were the stats that Kagami spent the last four years developing.

But as he tabbed over to the equipment list on the status screen, his hope evaporated.

The avatar was clearly wearing Danblf's bespoke wizarding gear—one-of-a-kind and commissioned by the King of Alcait upon Danblf's ascendance to the role of Elder of Summoning. Each piece was specially ordered and produced by other players who were craftsmen of renown. Only the dignified personage of Danblf would have access to those items; that was the problem.

At any prior point, it would have been the elegant, refined personage of Danblf, resplendent in his robes. But just like the mirror image in the knight captain's armor, a beautiful young lady stared back from the status screen.

Convinced this had to be some sort of mistake, she grasped the hem of her robe and pulled it over her head. The corresponding equipment line on her status screen changed to *None*. Letting the robe hang in one hand, she began to check over her now-exposed body as her silky silver hair fluttered in the breeze.

Her pert breasts were just a handful, and she had fair, almost translucent skin. A modest butt sat atop a pair of shapely legs. This was absolutely the female avatar Kagami had created with the Vanity Case.

"Whoaaa! Whoa, whoa, whoa! What are you doing?!" Having finished issuing orders to his subordinates, the captain turned to find the woman naked and oblivious. In a single graceful motion, he swept his red cloak around her shoulders. The rest of the knights within eyeshot exercised steely self-control and hastily turned their backs on the scandalous display.

Well, this seems like a bit of an overreaction from the NPCs, thought the woman.

Skilled players could acquire a retinue of NPC followers, and she'd assumed that was the case here. She had taken the knight captain for a player, but either the rest of the knights were players as well or the AI had gotten a significant upgrade during last night's patch.

"Come on!" the captain admonished. "A proper young lady should know better than to go around exposing herself like that. You're lucky that you've found yourself in the company of noble, honest knights. The world is full of people who might take advantage of you in such a state. You shouldn't let your guard down, miss."

More troublingly, their reaction settled the matter: he was now a *she*. It seemed that somehow, some way, she had screwed up and completed the character change. She needed to wrap this episode up and fork out another thousand yen to fix the problem before anyone caught on to what she'd done.

A frown stole over her face. Still covered by the knight captain's cloak, she replaced her robes and checked the status screen to make sure her avatar was no longer naked. Then she passed the cape back to the captain.

"Is that a User's Bangle? Is she an adventurer?" he muttered, glancing at the woman's arm while reattaching the cloak to his shoulders.

A User's Bangle? she asked herself. *What is he talking about?*

The captain was clearly looking her wrist terminal, but she'd never heard the term before. If he was a commander, especially the commander of an elite unit like the Magic-Clad Knights, then he obviously must've been a veteran player. But since all players would have a wrist terminal, why would that be a surprise to him? With every answer, more questions bubbled to the surface.

"If you are asking me if I'm an adventurer, well, of course I am." As confusing as the situation was, she knew *that* at least was completely true.

Her voice was still shocking to her ears. The cute, lilting tone mixed with Danblf's verbal tics had a dissonant effect that made her wince.

The Voice was part of Danblf's roleplaying shtick. Kagami figured such a dignified-looking character should have an equally dignified voice. And after four years of playing and speaking in such a way, it was a habit that came as naturally as logging in.

Even though that cadence didn't fit her current avatar, the thought of modifying how she spoke was strange and uncomfortable. She began to ponder how she should talk now that she was a woman, but she abandoned that train of thought quickly since there were more pressing matters at hand.

"I see. So you are an adventurer," the knight captain confirmed to himself. "Well, we appreciate your help, young miss. But can I ask about that black knight? I've never seen anything like it. What sort of technique did you use?"

"What do you mean? It's clearly just a summoning skill."

The woman followed this statement by resummoning her Evocation: Dark Knight, causing the minion to reappear beside her. The surrounding knights were unsettled by its oppressive aura, but the captain stared with great interest. He gawked at the black knight and the ominous presence that surrounded it, standing in stark contrast to the woman's own delicate appearance.

"Summoning! How marvelous. And it's an armor spirit... How rare." Lost in thought, the captain stared at the black knight, circling around it and inspecting its grand stature.

There were two types of spirits used by summoners. Primordial spirits were strong but difficult to locate and subdue, while manmade spirits, found within human creations, were easier to handle and tame.

A lesser summoning technique could be used to call manmade spirits forth from armor—the armor of those who had waged war would produce Dark Knights, and the armor of those who had died protecting the innocent produced Holy Knights. While it was a nominally easy spell, Danblf's continued use of the Dark Knight had honed it into a swordsman who could rival top-tier summoned spirits.

It seemed strange that the captain would consider such a rudimentary summoning technique to be a rare sight. Summoners used low-level techniques all the time. It would be rarer to find someone who'd never seen it before.

"I wonder when the request for assistance went out," said the captain. "Don't misunderstand me, miss—we're grateful for the help with these hordes appearing so frequently. It would have been nice to know you were going to join us, though."

The captain's complaint was belied by his happy expression. It was clear that the knights had their hands full with this fight, but his comment added more layers of mystery to the situation. First, monster hordes were normally dealt with by whichever of the Nine Wise Men was on duty that day, no knightly backup necessary. Secondly, monster hordes weren't that frequent.

"Hrmm, but these attacks only happen once a month. That doesn't seem like too much to handle."

Perhaps some people considered that too frequent, but she was getting another vibe from this conversation. It was as if there was some fundamental difference in worldview between her and the captain.

"Once a month? Maybe that was the case ten years ago. We've had *three* incursions in the past four weeks." The captain gave her a skeptical look, then turned glumly back to the Dark Knight, looking the summon over like he was comparing their physiques.

"Did you say...ten years ago?" That was the red flag she'd been searching for. Time in *AEO* moved at the same rate as time on Earth. Ten years ago would have been six years before the game entered open beta mode.

"Come now, miss! I'm sure an adventurer already knows the stories—the war against the demons that fell from the sky and the Defense of the Three Great Kingdoms. Monster horde appearances have doubled since then."

"The Defense of the Three Great Kingdoms, you say? I've never heard of that."

"Really? Huh. Well, I guess you would have been just a child—too young to be adventuring."

She opened her system terminal in search of answers. A screen popped up and she began navigating through the menus. To the knights, she appeared to simply poke at the empty air in front of her, as if shooing away gnats. The captain patiently waited for her to say something as a confused look spread across her face.

She ignored the comprehensive timeline displayed in the *History* tab, instead staring speechlessly at a single entry at the top of the list.

Ark Calendar Year 2146, April 23rd, it said. *The second prince of the Kingdom of Milston was born. He was named Atolzard.*

The birth announcement wasn't what shocked her. Panicked, her eyes flicked to the top left where the current time and date were displayed.

Ark Calendar Year 2146, May 12th, 3:12 p.m.

"What day is it?" she demanded, staring into the captain's face.

"It's Wednesday, m'lady."

"No, no, no! What year, month, and day is it?"

"Oh." The knight captain withdrew and opened a silver pocket watch. "It's May 12th, 2146."

The game had begun in the year 2112.

It wasn't a bug; the knight captain's answer matched the one shown on her system screen. Unless the dev team had decided to skip a few decades of time on the in-game clocks, thirty years had elapsed since Kagami passed out.

She scanned through the timeline, and an endless string of unremembered historical events scrolled past. Sure enough, on June 20th, 2136, an event called *Defense of the Three Great Kingdoms* was logged.

Grasping a lock of her silvery hair, she held it up to her nose. She inhaled deeply, smelling the faint vanilla-like scent of a sweet shampoo. Then she put the hair in her mouth. It was largely tasteless, but her tongue and lips could feel each individual strand.

If full five-senses VR had been patched into the game, the patch notes would have been documented somewhere on the timeline. The two prior updates were still listed in the history files, along with documentation, but there was no mention of an upgrade beyond that point.

The mystery grew deeper and more troubling.

She began to question her earlier assumptions. Why could she suddenly taste the grass and sniff the air? Would technology like this really make a surprise debut in a video game? How could it be this flawless in its detail and execution?

It all seemed completely impossible, and yet her senses weren't lying.

That left one highly improbable option. One that she didn't want to believe was true.

The woman closed the menu and looked squarely at the captain, who had grown even more perplexed by her strange behavior.

"Ah! I realize we haven't properly met, miss. My name is Graia Astol, Captain of the Magic-Clad Knights' First Squadron." Captain Graia added a slight bow to the end of his introduction. His eyes were full of interest as he stared back at the woman. "And while it's evident that you are a skilled mage, I still do not know who you are. Would you do me the favor of introducing yourself, miss?"

Who didn't know about Danblf, one of the Wise Men of Alcait, for whom even the label of sublime seemed insufficient? More uncertainty arose.

Introducing yourself upon meeting someone, and asking their name in return, was a natural thing to do in most cases. But that only applied in the real world, not in the game. When a player opened an inspection window, the inspected player's name was automatically displayed floating above their avatar. There was no need to have a discussion about it, and yet Graia had introduced himself and asked her name in turn.

"Why not merely Inspect me?" Something else was going on, and she posed her response as a test against a new hypothesis.

"Hmm..." Graia peered a little more closely at her, searching for some hidden clue to the riddle. "Well, you're quite skilled, young miss, but I'm afraid I cannot deduce your identity. I apologize. Does anyone else here recognize her?"

The knights present shook their heads and shrugged, saying they didn't know who she was either.

"Hrmmm, I see..." She knew some players considered it impolite to Inspect other players without express permission, sort of a roleplaying tic, but even those players should have been willing to take a peek once permission was granted. The captain and his knights should have known instantly that she was Danblf, despite the change in appearance.

Yet not a single one recognized her. The only conclusion she could draw was that the knights around her were unable to use the Inspect function, including the knight captain.

"None of them can use basic game mechanics," the woman muttered to herself, hand on her chin. With this new information, she began forming yet another hypothesis.

"Ah...I do apologize, miss. As you can see, we are but simple swordsmen and unfamiliar with adventurers and magic." Graia mistook the woman's silence for shock at not being recognized. His fellow knights also appeared apologetic and slightly embarrassed, which just made her theory that they were individuals with agency seem more likely.

They seemed real in every way, but they obviously weren't NPCs *or* players. VR might be advanced, but it simply wasn't capable of anything this complex. She had no choice but to abandon the idea that this was some sort of software update.

Slowly but surely, she kept coming back to an old urban legend. It seemed impossible, but with all the evidence stacking in its favor, it was also impossible to completely deny.

What if this is real? The thought was ludicrous, but another thought struck her immediately. *Oh, hell! I should have tried that first.*

There was one absolutely certain way to prove this was just a game. She could log out and just quit the game.

She tried to flip to the system tab but...she couldn't do it. The entire system menu had disappeared. Even giving the force-quit command to force the VR set to reboot wasn't working.

Evidence was growing that she was inside some sort of alternate reality. That just led her to question if this was the same *AEO* world that she knew and loved.

"Sir, have you heard of a man by the name Danblf?" she asked with trepidation.

"Well, of course! I reckon everyone in the kingdom knows about Master Danblf," Graia answered with a note of pride. He looked around to his men, seeking agreement, and they all nodded as if it was the easiest question they'd ever answered.

"I see. So he is known to you. Good." But had this Danblf been Kagami's character, or just some historical figure with the same name? "And what sort of person was Danblf?"

"What sort of person?" Graia cocked his head to the side. "Well, obviously, he was known to all throughout the kingdom. Master Danblf was associated with the Age of Strife almost thirty years ago—a true hero of the nation. Known as Danblf the One-Man

Army, other countries trembled before his summoning powers. He was also one of the Elders of the Linked Silver Towers."

He said it so matter-of-factly, and it fell perfectly in line with her memories, even down to the hokey nickname.

"Hmm... A hero, you say."

"Indeed! In the war that followed our nation's founding, he held off an entire enemy army, it's said! The Elders formed their own unit and led a daring assault that plunged the enemy camp into confusion and chaos. I've also heard that he created refining techniques that few users can master even today. And he wielded the strongest of the immortal Sage arts! The tales of the Wise Men are legendary."

All this fit perfectly with her own history—the tales of war, her Dual Class of Sage, even the refining techniques. Folk tales of herself, or of Danblf, were clearly being passed down.

"Hrmmm, I see. And what of Danblf's final moments?" Her decisions from this point forward hinged on the answer to a single question.

"Final moments? Huh. I don't think I ever heard about him dying, actually... If I recall correctly, he ventured out to the border to take care of a monster incursion about thirty years ago and was never seen again. There was no way Master Danblf would have fallen to a rabble like that, so a manhunt was held throughout the kingdom. He was never found."

"I see. As I thought."

The missing link had been found. She was now convinced that this was somehow the same world, just thirty years in the future. She wasn't sure how the game had become reality, but she forced herself to calm down and stop worrying.

The pressing matter of the moment was whether or not to claim that she was Danblf. The name was famous across the land. He was known for his elegant, dignified appearance; for his battle prowess and summoning powers; and for being an Elder of the Linked Silver Towers.

And that legendary hero was now...an adorable young lady.

If a woman suddenly appeared claiming to be a male hero who disappeared thirty years ago, no one would take her seriously without a lengthy explanation. Even if she tried to convince people she was telling the truth they'd just ask for an explanation. And there was no way she could just admit she was fooling around with a Vanity Case to create the ideal female form. It would be certain career suicide for Danblf's public persona to admit to something like that.

Just imagining the looks she'd get when she regained her former form made her break into a cold sweat. This was a scandal of immeasurable proportion.

Her only option was deception. If Graia and his fellow knights couldn't use the Inspect function, then she had a leg up already. Decision made, and with no one else the wiser, she grinned to herself.

"Well, then, as to the question of my name. I am...Mira." That alias seemed as good as any—a little white lie for the sake of protecting her honor. "Naturally, you wouldn't have heard of me yet, as I'm new around here."

CHAPTER 2

As she spoke, her hand went to her chin to stroke Danblf's beard, but all she felt was the uncanny smoothness of her porcelain skin.

She
Professed
Herself
Pupil of the
Wise Man

A GREAT PYRE was soon lit on the field beside Mierte Forest, and the knights fed the goblin corpses into the flames. The smoke belching forth was black as pitch, a hellish miasma crawling its way skyward. Graia and Mira conversed as they watched the men work. Without complaint, the knights cleaned up the mess she had created.

"Lady Mira, eh? I'll make sure to remember that. I never expected a *summoner* to be so powerful."

"Surely this isn't anything out of the ordinary."

"Sure, they were just goblins." Graia shook his head, gazing at the Dark Knight standing by Mira's side. "But to have slain them so quickly...and at such a young age! You must have had an amazing teacher."

"Hrmmm, well, I suppose I did." Another white lie. She hadn't had a teacher, but it was certainly easier than coming up with a complete cover story on the spot.

"News, sir!" said a knight rushing up to Graia. "The escaped monster has yet to be found. One of the pursuit groups has returned, but we'll continue our search."

"I see. I've never seen such a creature before. Shame that it got away. Continue the search while the rest of us finish cleaning up." Report received, Graia summoned another knight to deliver a message to their garrison. The runner eyed the Dark Knight with trepidation, and the captain noticed. "What do you think? This here's a Dark Knight, a summoned armor spirit."

Graia beamed at the spirit almost as if he had summoned it himself.

"A summon, sir? Those are quite rare. I've heard of armor spirits, but I never imagined them to be so...intimidating."

"Indeed! It surprised me as well."

Mira eavesdropped on their conversation, certain parts piquing her interest. Had summoners really become so rare? To be sure, the class was less popular than others—especially when compared to Priests, who specialized in recovery and support techniques. Those guys were indispensable when forming a party. But still, summoning hadn't been uncommon.

Maybe the steep learning curve had dissuaded others from pursuing summoning during the intervening years. Back then, mage classes started with minimal skills, and summoners got Contract Forging. It had no inherent offensive or defensive power and could only be used on defeated spirits, allowing a young mage to use them as summoned pets.

Summoners were incredibly powerful in the end game, but the early days were brutal. The catch was that if a summoner wanted to bind a spirit, they had to do all the damage themselves. No asking a friend or hiring a mercenary to whittle it down first—the summoner had to deal every point of damage. Many people avoided the class entirely after reading about the difficulties on the message boards.

But Danblf had stuck it out. After stocking up on large amounts of recovery items and explosives, Danblf spent two hours at the Ancient Yubeladius Battleground pummeling armor spirits until he finally bound a spirit in a contract. That was the Dark Knight, and since then, they'd forged a deep and lasting relationship as master and minion.

In many ways, his success served as an advertisement for the class. Others flocked to become summoners because they admired Danblf and read about his exploits on the forums. Mira worried that without her presence over the past thirty years, the class might have taken a nosedive. It had been a long time; a lot could have happened.

"Pardon, I was hoping you might be able to answer a few questions." Mira took the opportunity to pump Graia for as much information as she could while the knights continued to clear the battlefield.

"Well, thanks for the chat, and take care on your way back."

"That's normally my line. But after seeing you in battle, Lady Mira, I'm not sure it's necessary!" Graia gave a hearty laugh and offered his right hand. "This has certainly been entertaining. I hope next time we meet, you'll put those skills to use and give my men even more cleanup work to do!"

"Hrmmm. I'll see what I can do." Mira smiled at Graia's half-joking tone, taking the proffered hand.

"Heh, we'll be waiting." And with that, Graia and his men set off toward home, the marching cadence of the knights echoing in their wake.

Mira stood in the scorched field and tried to process the information she'd learned. Graia had been an open book, taking the time to answer each and every question she threw at him. Most had been about the current state of affairs in the Kingdom of Alcait.

It seemed that Danblf wasn't the only Elder who vanished thirty years prior. Eight of the Nine Wise Men were missing. One by one, they disappeared within a year of Danblf. While their deputies and scholars tried their best, they lacked the raw magic power of the tower Elders and were stretched to their limits trying to carry out their responsibilities. The kingdom was largely defenseless.

Fortunately, at least one of their number—Master Wizard Luminaria, the Natural Disaster—reappeared inexplicably ten years after her disappearance. Before that return, the loss of the Elders had remained a secret known only to the upper echelons of the government. It was at Luminaria's urging that a formal public announcement was made.

Elder Luminaria. There was a name that Mira knew well. They were both mages and had maintained a friendly rivalry since the game launched.

Luminaria's avatar featured long, strikingly crimson hair. She was tall and busty, with stunning looks to put any model to shame—the very object of men's desire. And since she was played by a man, their conversations were frank, dirty, and full of unfiltered guy talk.

Honestly, remembering those talks while looking like she did now made Mira feel a little uncomfortable. But it sounded like Luminaria had disappeared thirty years previous, just like Danblf—or rather, her character did. And then she mysteriously reappeared a long time later, just like Danblf did, despite the hiccup with his appearance. But the similarities were uncanny.

Luminaria was a friend, and as a player, she might have gone through the same thing. Perhaps she'd be able to clue Mira in on what was going on.

Her next stop: the Sacred City of Silverhorn, home of the Nine Linked Silver Towers, where magical knowledge from across the continent was gathered.

As Mira left the field and headed down the forest road toward Silverhorn, the sky peeking through the treetops began to darken, vermillion mixing with the blue. Checking the time in the status menu, she saw it was just past five in the evening.

If she recalled correctly, Silverhorn was nearly an hour's journey on foot from the field, and she hadn't even covered half the distance yet. The reason was simple: she'd been taking too many detours. From engrossing herself in watching the butterflies draw nectar from flowers to observing earthworms dig their way through the soil, the realism and ambiance of this familiar-yet-new world stimulated her curiosity to the point of distraction.

Mira closed the status menu and felt a pang of hunger. Remembering an apple pie that had been in her Item Box, she touched the icon, and it suddenly appeared in her hand as if by magic.

Her eyes narrowed as she stared at the pie. It had been in her inventory for at least a week of subjective time, and she had objectively purchased it over thirty years ago, by current reckoning.

But it *looked* fine.

Hesitantly, she brought the pie closer to her face and took a sniff. The sweet scent of vanilla and spice filled her nose, and her stomach let out a gurgle. Mind made up, Mira opened wide and took a big bite. The flaky texture of the pastry and the sweet, tart flavor of the apple instantly filled her mouth, stimulating her taste buds. Mira had never even tasted an apple pie in the real world before that moment, but she was sure that it was the most delectable thing she'd ever eaten.

Encouraged by that success, she opened her Item Box again and withdrew an apple au lait. The beverage was a perennial favorite among the mage classes. Blending milk and apple, the creamy, pale amber drink increased the mana regeneration speed.

She brought it to her mouth. "Delicious..."

The praise slipped from her lips. The textures and flavors of both foods were perfect, and she swallowed both down without issue.

She sighed softly as she gazed at the sky, watching the clouds drift by and taking in the world with all her senses. The feeling of the wind teasing her hair, the living scent of the forest, the fatigue that came from physical exertion. And the taste of the pie and the apple au lait.

The simple realness couldn't be denied. The more information she gathered and the more she considered her situation, the more difficult it became to believe that this *wasn't* reality.

Mira decided to accept it as a fact.

She would act on the premise that the world around her was real. If it turned out that she was wrong, then no harm done. This would just be a funny story to tell later. But if she acted as if this weren't real, she might unwittingly do something irreversible—death might actually mean death—with no hope of revival. And hanging someone out to dry might come back to bite her later.

But one problem at a time. She needed to find Luminaria. Her friend had been living in this world for twenty years and might know what happened. With renewed focus, Mira set off down the trail to Silverhorn.

Something with an ashen gray body, fierce eyes, and saliva dripping from its razor-sharp fangs appeared before Mira. She recognized the beast as it made a growling approach.

It was a Saber Dog, one of the first beasts new players encountered in *AEO*.

Saber Dogs were a common predator, quite clever and vicious. This particular specimen measured over a meter from tip to tail and was a dangerous foe for even full-grown adults. And here it had found a weak little girl who had wandered too far from the village with no one around to protect her. Mira's robe might hint that she was some form of mage, but no matter—she looked like a defenseless girl, in over her head. The hunter confidently closed the gap between itself and this easy prey.

Even wild dogs shouldn't judge a book by its cover.

Mira struck. Her right hand moved through the air with lightning speed, and the Saber Dog's eyes filled with terror a moment before its body crumpled. Blood splatters bloomed on the surrounding trees like grim flowers, and tufts of burning fur burst into the air.

The second-rank Sage skill, Immortal Arts, Heaven: Shock Wave, projected a wave of kinetic force in front of her strike. For a mage of her caliber, it was like a delete button for low-level monsters. She already knew that she could use her summoning abilities, but she had been looking for an excuse to make sure her Sage techniques were still available to her.

"Check that one off the list."

Marveling at the scent of burning hair, Mira turned and continued on her way without another look back.

4

THE SUN SET and countless stars shone in the evening sky. They were just as she remembered, and the sight drew a small sigh of admiration.

Finally reaching Silverhorn, Mira waved to the gatekeeper as she passed through—only to be dumbstruck by the changes to the city since last she saw it. She had good reason. The walls surrounding the city had grown taller and larger, and the city sprawled beyond them, taking up three times as much land as she remembered. The only proof that this was the location of her in-game home were the nine spires looming over the town. The Linked Silver Towers symbolized the city and stood as a regal reminder of the magic at the settlement's center.

"Well, It's been thirty years, after all," Mira muttered with a hint of melancholy. She headed off down a main street toward the tower complex, pushing her way through a crowd of locals heading home from work.

Lit by the moonlight and the flickering flames of the streetlamps, her youthful appearance made her seem out of place in the blue-collar crowd, and she drew the attention of the people around her. Some worried about the young lady walking alone so late at night, while others were dazzled by her mysterious beauty. Mira passed by, unaware of the reactions caused by her accidental avatar.

Whether she knew it or not, the knights she'd met on the battlefield deserved commendations for being able to endure such beauty without being enthralled by her charms.

As she reached the end of the street, Mira found her path blocked by a tall wall and a heavy gate. Within stood the majestic shapes of the Linked Silver Towers, bathed in the moonlight. She craned her neck to look up at them.

To get to the Tower of Evocation, she would have to pass through the gate. But to prevent outsiders from entering, special certification was required—one either needed a pass, issued by a Linked Silver Tower administrator and only valid for a limited number of uses; a Silver Key, issued to tower researchers; or a Master Key, of which there were only nine and which were solely possessed by the tower Elders.

No guards stood watch over the automated gate, and the grounds beyond the entrance were largely deserted. For an Elder like Mira, the gate shouldn't pose any problem... But as she moved toward the gate, she noticed something awry.

Instead of swinging open like an automatic door, it stood

motionless and resolute to prevent her entrance. She nearly walked into it face-first before hurriedly taking a step back and staring in disbelief.

"What is the meaning of this?!"

Mira stared up at the gate as she paced back and forth before it, jumped up and down a few times, and tried moving closer and further away to see if she could get it to activate. The gate remained steadfast, staring down at her impassively like an unimpressed child watching an unfunny clown.

"Hmm, odd," mumbled Mira, thinking back to what she knew about the gate.

It required a key, and as the Elder of the Tower of Evocation, she naturally held a Master Key. She opened her Item Box and switched to the tab containing her special items. After scrolling through the countless array of item icons, she found her Master Key and withdrew it. It didn't look like a medieval key; it was more of a silver keycard with the nine towers engraved on it. One shone a brilliant gold, corresponding to the Tower of Evocation and indicating the Elder of Summoning to whom it belonged.

The key wasn't damaged as far as she could tell. As Mira puzzled over the situation, she leaned forward, and the gate swung open.

"Ho ho! So that's how it works."

She returned the Master Key to her Item Box and the gate swung closed again. And as she withdrew the key, it opened. Once upon a time, the gate worked as long as the key was in the player's Item Box. Now the gate seemed to only recognize the key when it was held. This mystery solved, Mira repeated the action several times, opening and closing the gate on a whim.

Having received satisfaction, she passed through and returned the Master Key to her Item Box.

Thirty years had elapsed since Mira last walked here, and she was concerned that she might not recognize Danblf's former home. The grounds beneath the towers were covered in a grassy lawn, and she saw a few researchers hurriedly moving between the tower entrances. It was well after dusk, but they didn't seem to keep regular hours. Mages would be mages, no matter the time period. Her worries were unfounded and she heaved a sigh that was half relief, half exasperation.

The nine towers were arranged in a wide circle around the grounds. Clockwise from the main gate were the Tower of Sorcery, the Tower of the Holy, the Tower of Divination, the Tower of Exorcism, the Tower of Evocation, the Tower of Necromancy, the Tower of Immortality, the Tower of Demonology, and the Tower of the Ethereal.

Luminaria was the Elder of Sorcery, which meant that, if she was truly here, she would no doubt be in the Elder's chambers of the closest tower. Mira moved toward the tower entrance, causing a stir among the mages who caught sight of the young woman walking with a purpose. They cocked their heads in confusion as she passed by.

The towers themselves didn't require any sort of key, so Mira strolled right in to the spacious atrium at the building's base.

The tower was made up of numerous ring-shaped facilities stacked one atop another, all connected by a spiral staircase that climbed upward.

The entire tower had been built by players and enlarged over the years, as more people needed space to research and work. Now it stood a full thirty stories high—far too tall to climb using just the stairs. An elevator powered by Ethereal techniques had been rigged up in the center of the atrium.

The elevator differed from one found on Earth. It consisted of a thin circular stone inscribed with magic circles that floated upward and downward within a transparent tube. Each floor was connected to the elevator via a covered walkway. When viewed from the ground floor, the whole arrangement resembled a fish skeleton.

The Ethereal school of magic was perplexing and difficult to master, but it was also the type of magic most often seen in practical use. The techniques could be used for a variety of purposes, including lighting, power, and more. The only limit was the players' ingenuity.

The tower's elevator had been born from the collective knowledge of many players working together to build something amazing. That cooperative dynamic was baked into the core of *Ark Earth Online*.

Mira looked up and remembered how things used to be.

Upon starting the game, players could choose to start out in one of the Initial Three Kingdoms. Citizens of a Kingdom didn't lose their items upon death, could recover from ailments with just a few minutes' rest, and faced only minor tolls when traveling. Additionally, they could use any facilities offered by their Kingdom for free. In return, they were charged a nominal income tax that paid for those privileges. The allure of citizenship was obvious.

But after reaching a certain rank, players were exiled from their starting nation. Those who no longer belonged to a Kingdom faced various hardships, such as a harsh death penalty that stripped a player of all their owned items and left them too weak to fight for an entire twenty-four-hour period.

The extreme way in which players were expelled from their starting countries initially garnered a fair bit of criticism on the forums. However, as open beta wore on, there was a grudging acceptance of the mechanic as "just part of the game."

As people began to accept their new roles as wanderers and vagabonds, the first nation builders appeared. By setting up player-managed countries, they made it possible to still enjoy the benefits of belonging to a Kingdom even after leaving the Initial Three.

This resulted in a land rush, which then evolved into a series of wars over territory. Would-be kings of these fledgling countries began hiring armies by offering high pay to citizens who agreed to join the fray. The price was worth it; a veteran player could be as effective as ten NPC soldiers.

From those prototype nations, regional superpowers arose. Their populations of player-citizens kept increasing; their stockpiles of money and top-level players made it easy to win battles. The larger nations began to spread across the continent, and the gap between the large kingdoms and smaller countries grew. Newly established countries found themselves invaded or made into puppet states. The world slowly became inaccessible to newcomers.

In order to stabilize the political situation, the various player kings came together to establish a treaty based on a set of metrics known as the National Power Rankings.

Nations were ranked on a three-point scale: territory held, economic power, and military strength. This score would limit how many players could participate in battles, with the lower-scoring nation setting the cap. Furthermore, there were two pools that battle participants could be drawn from, citizens and mercenaries, and a further restriction dictated that at least 70 percent of the chosen participants had to be citizens.

This made it easier to balance national strength, increased the value of NPC soldiers, and gave individual players the chance to greatly affect the outcome of history.

But the system wasn't perfect. This caused countries to value citizens that were combat-effective even at lower ranks. Young players who had chosen mage classes could only use their beginner skills and were seen as a burden.

This led to a common belief that mages as a whole were an evolutionary dead end. With the ratification of the treaty, an entire class of players was left without a purpose or a place. It was assumed that a mage chosen for one of the valuable national battle slots could snatch defeat from the jaws of victory.

And so, wizards, summoners, and the rest of the mages became players without a home.

The Kingdom of Alcait, located in the southeastern region of the continent, was a small country born in this period of warfare. It was protected by the treaty's ban on waging war against new countries until four months past their founding. This kept the new nation safe for the time being, but despite the lack of a major power in the area, they were surrounded by other small- and medium-sized kingdoms. The clock was ticking, and they'd soon be easy pickings.

Solomon, King of Alcait, had a plan. He was well acquainted with the hardship that mage-class players faced and knew their aspirations and potential. At a time when the status of mages was uncertain at best, Solomon invited Danblf to join his country. The news spread, and magic users heard that there was a country willing to accept them. One after another, they immigrated to Alcait seeking fair treatment and opportunity. As they gathered into the kingdom, an interesting phenomenon occurred.

The mages began to share information. This was a novel approach in a game where learning a skill that no one else knew was an absolute way to gain an edge. Information fetched a high price, but the gathered mages shared their techniques with each other freely.

Solomon worried that the inevitable war would destroy his

kingdom, but his people were not willing to give up. To protect the Kingdom of Alcait, they cast aside their own individual aspirations. They joined together in search of collective strength, and Solomon saw the path to victory.

After independence was secured, a city in the kingdom's territory was dedicated to the research of magic techniques. Nine facilities were built—one for each school of magic. These were the foundations of what would become the Linked Silver Towers, and the small Kingdom of Alcait gave birth to an elite cadre of mages that could withstand the invasion forces of even the mightiest nations.

But that all happened over thirty years ago. Lost in the emotions of those memories, Mira entered the elevator to pay a visit to the Elder of Sorcery's chambers on the uppermost floor.

She
Professed
Herself
Pupil of the
Wise Man

THE TRANSPARENT DOORS to the elevator parted, and Mira exited. Crossing the translucent pathway that connected the elevator shaft to the floor, she entered a circular hallway that led to each room of the Elder's chambers: a private room, a laboratory, an office, and a room for her attendant. She stood at the door to the laboratory.

"Hey! Luminaria! Are you here?! Anybody home?!" Mira pounded on the door with her tiny fist. The hallway filled with the echo of her high voice and the thuds of the abused door.

This was the most likely place to find her, since Luminaria spent most of her game time tucked away within her laboratory. Mira pounded away, waiting for her friend to kick the door open with her standard *"Give it a break already!"*

"No dice. Maybe she's out?" Mira stopped her assault to listen at the door. On the rare occasion that Luminaria couldn't be found in her laboratory, she was usually in a nearby forest conducting some crackpot experiment. "Typical. Just when I need her most."

Mira let out another sigh and placed a hand on her chin, wondering what to do next. She paced back and forth, debating if she should wait around for Luminaria to return.

"And who might you be?" a familiar voice said.

Turning, Mira saw a beautiful woman dressed in a secretary's attire, with shoulder-length blonde hair and blue eyes behind her glasses. Luminaria's attendant stared at Mira with suspicion.

"Long time no see, Lythalia. Would you perchance know Luminaria's whereabouts?"

Upon attaining the rank of Elder, a player's country granted them an NPC character to assist with their research and other miscellaneous tasks. Luminaria's assistant, Lythalia, happened to be an elf.

The long-lived race retained their beauty for hundreds of years and were considered mystical beings by many. Elves were an NPC-only race, one of a wide variety of NPC races including dwarves, gnomes, sirens, werewolves, and giants—as well as the Miao, which looked almost identical to humans except for their cat ears and tails, and the mighty Galidia, marked by their strong, robust forms.

"Who might you be, miss? The only access to this floor is via the elevator. Are you authorized to be here?" The air grew thick with tension, and Lythalia's eyes were filled with caution.

"Well, the thing is...ah. I see the issue..."

The fact that she now inhabited the small body of a lady instead of the grand figure of Danblf was once again causing problems for Mira. It was clear that Lythalia couldn't use the

Inspect command to ascertain her true identity, or else the jig would already be up.

There was no guarantee that Lythalia would believe Mira if she claimed to be Danblf. And honestly, Mira wasn't sure she could handle the shame of being seen in her current form by someone who knew her from before—even if that person had been an NPC at the time. Mira couldn't bear the idea of Lythalia judging her for cavorting around in the form of a young woman.

Luminaria was the only one she could tell.

After all, the sorceress was a connoisseur of...*this sort of thing*. After having seen Luminaria in a similar state countless times, Mira was confident that she would consider Mira's situation adorable, not scandalous. But that didn't help with the current misunderstanding.

Lythalia was correct that not just anyone should be able to use that elevator. Mira only knew the method because she was an Elder, of course. There was probably no way for Mira to pass herself off as a simple summoner stopping by to gawk at the Elder's Chambers.

She had to think fast. What convenient excuse would justify her presence and her knowledge of the elevator...and allow her to come and go as freely as she'd like in the future? And could she pull that off without spilling the beans that she was Danblf?

Suddenly, inspiration struck.

"Tell me, ma'am, do you know of Danblf?" asked Mira, as she gave Lythalia her most confident smile.

"Certainly! He's the Elder of the Tower of Evocation," Lythalia replied immediately, a bit of composure returning to her voice.

"That's right. And I'm Danblf's, um, pupil. And he, uh, hath bidden me to deliver a message to Lumi…Lady Luminaria in his stead. That's what I'm here to do." As the lies fell from Mira's mouth, her expression never faltered. But she searched Lythalia's face for any clue that the elf might have cottoned on to the ruse.

The moment Mira claimed a connection to Danblf, a wave of mixed emotions passed across Lythalia's face—an understandable reaction for someone hearing that the apprentice of a Wise Man who'd been missing for the past thirty years was standing on her doorstep.

"Master Danblf…?! Well, then, of course! But I heard nothing about Master Danblf taking on a pupil."

"Well, yes. I only became his pupil recently."

"Recently?! Does that mean that Master Danblf has returned to us?!" Lythalia's eyes sparkled as she stalked towards Mira.

Faced with such fervor, cracks began to form in Mira's mask of deceit. "Y-yes. But alas, he is unable to come himself. Which is why he sent me."

"I see. Poor Master Danblf… What on earth could be keeping him from returning to us?"

"Well, you see, it's like…"

The plan would be perfect if Lythalia would stop asking for details. Another idea came to Mira; just let Danblf be Danblf.

"He is training a new summon and as such has sequestered himself within the Mystic City of Beasts."

She hoped Lythalia would fall for it. The Mystic City of Beasts was a famous hunting ground for players. Situated in the abandoned ruins of an ancient city, it was now overrun by a veritable zoo of monsters and phantasms. As players defeated monsters within the city, they gained increasing stacks of blessings. The blessings increased a player's experience point gain, recovery rate, and the drop rate of rare items from enemies.

But as soon as a player left the city, all blessings would reset. It was common practice to stock up on consumable items and stay inside for as long as humanly possible.

"Another new summon? He never changes! Always disappearing off to the Mystic City to tamper with some spirit or another. Oh, Master Danblf. I do wish to see him again." From the way Lythalia was nodding, it seemed she bought it.

Crisis averted. And it served as further proof for Mira that her past actions were clearly part of the history of this world.

"Indeed, that's how it is. Now then, about Lumi...Lady Luminaria?"

"Oh, right. Mistress Luminaria is currently... No. I mustn't. I can't." Although hearing that Danblf might be alive had lit up her face with hope, Lythalia was quick to restore her composure to prim professionalism. "Certainly, that sounds like Master Danblf, but how can I be sure? What if you're just pretending to be his pupil? Do you have any proof of your claim?"

"Proof? Hrmmm..." mumbled Mira, patting herself down in search of an answer that would put this inquisition to bed. "Would this do the trick?"

Mira reached into her Item Box for something that only Danblf would have possessed—a silver card engraved with nine towers.

"That...that's the Master Key for the Tower of Evocation! Then you really are Master Danblf's... I'm sorry, may I have your name, please?" A smile bloomed across Lythalia's face.

"My name is Mira. My master has told me all about you, Miss Lythalia. Is Lady Luminaria not here at the moment?"

"That's correct. Mistress Luminaria is presently at Lunatic Lake. She won't be back until late tomorrow."

"I see. Well, nothing I can do about that. I'll have to try again later." Mira frowned. Traveling all the way to Lunatic Lake would be far too much of a hassle tonight. Besides, what was waiting one night compared to thirty years of missing time?

"Look at the time!" Lythalia drew in close like a cat stalking its prey. "You can stay here until Mistress Luminaria returns if you'd like. Seeing as it's already evening, why not spend the night in my room? You can tell me all about what Master Danblf has been up to!"

Reflexively, Mira scurried backward until her back hit the door. Her expression stiffened and she couldn't bear to make eye contact with the elf. Hanging around here would involve creating more stories and excuses that would eventually give her away. Mira didn't feel like digging herself any deeper into that hole.

"My apologies, I still have other tasks to attend to on Master Danblf's behalf. I'll be back tomorrow." A quick, firm excuse. It was time to get out while the getting was good.

"Oh, that's too bad... Well perhaps not the entire night. Just a moment of your time, please, Miss Mira. Can't you tell me what happened thirty years ago? What has Master Danblf been doing all this time?"

"That will have to wait until tomorrow. My first priority must be the tasks my master hath assigned," Mira squawked. Shaking off the pursuing Lythalia, she dashed back to the elevator and began the descent back to ground level.

I've got to come up with a solid cover story for situations like this, she resolved. Regret filled her for the lies she had told, and a great sigh escaped her as she looked back up the elevator shaft to see Lythalia pressed to the side of transparent tube.

"She's a lot clingier now that she's not an NPC."

Before, she'd always seemed to be a hardworking secretary-type character. Had the change been instant, or was it a thirty-year process of personality evolution? Mira gave a wry smile as she stroked her chin with her hand and watched the floors pass by.

A few seconds later, she stepped out onto the first floor and gave an encouraging shout to the researchers bustling about the base of the tower. "Keep at it!"

It was the kind of thing she would have done back when she was Danblf. She didn't stop to observe the result of her action, but the sudden cheer from an unknown woman gave the researchers the drive to power through the night.

After leaving the Tower of Sorcery, Mira made her way to the Tower of Evocation. Luminaria might be returning tomorrow, but she still had matters to attend to. Her excuses to Lythalia hadn't been total lies. First and foremost, she needed to check the condition of her own Elder's chambers. Assuming everything was still in order, she could spend the night there.

The Tower of Evocation had the same layout as the Tower of Sorcery, and the silent interior was bright as day with swaying lights created by Ethereal techniques. As she made her way to the elevator and began to ascend, Mira squinted at the glare and made a mental note to dim the light levels.

Unlike the Tower of Sorcery, each level she passed was deserted. There wasn't a single researcher in sight. Clearly, the number of summoners in the kingdom had greatly decreased, and Mira thought back to how the knights had described summoning techniques as "rare."

Mira felt a pang of loss, like she was witnessing an old friend's final moments.

6

THE TOP FLOOR of the Tower of Evocation was largely the same as the penthouse in the Tower of Sorcery. Mira marched straight down the red-carpeted hallway from the elevator to her private chamber.

Long ago, Danblf had decorated the sides of the hall with black suits of armor done up in the same style as the Dark Knight. Sandwiched between two of them was the imposing black door to her quarters. Mira reached out for the handle before stopping, her hand a fraction of an inch away.

"Ah, right. Almost forgot."

She dug into her Item Box for the Master Key. She held it up to the door and heard the satisfying clunk of the lock releasing.

The doorknob was cold to the touch as she entered, which made her feel uneasy. This was such a familiar place to her, but she realized that this was the first time she'd *truly* entered her chambers.

Little details struck her. There was no shoe closet. Why would there be? Avatars never took their shoes off upon entering someone's home. But now this was reality, and traipsing into her living room with muddy shoes felt wrong. She took off her boots and looked around for a place to put them. Finding none, she let them fall to the foyer floor. Mira decided that was a problem for another day.

She walked barefoot into the familiar-yet-foreign room. Covering the floor was a massive rug made from the pelt of the Grand Caecus, Lord of the Beast—a memento of Danblf's past adventures. A chuckle escaped her as she remembered how the craftsman who made it pleaded with Danblf to use the rare and valuable pelt for something other than a rug. In the end, the craftsman relented, and now the shimmering golden fur caressed her feet as she paced around the room and took stock.

Other keepsakes lined the walls. But as Mira inspected them, she noticed that each one was in a different location from where she last remembered them.

"This must be Mariana's doing."

It had to be. No one besides Danblf and his attendant had access to these chambers, and since Danblf had been missing for thirty years, it narrowed down the list of suspects dramatically.

Mariana was a pathological organizer. Whenever Danblf returned home from hunting, he'd stuffed loot away randomly into the many storage closets around the top floor, only to find it carefully sorted, cleaned, and filed away when he next logged in. No matter the mess he left, Mariana would make it orderly right away.

While that was lovely, it was also frustrating. Mariana had a habit of changing the locations of things on a monthly basis, and that often meant that Danblf couldn't find the things he was looking for. Her internal sense of *feng shui* kept him guessing where important items might be on any given day.

But as adorable and irritating as Mariana could be, Mira couldn't help but feel saddened and guilty at the thought that her attendant had spent the past thirty years straightening and cleaning the rooms of a master who never came home. She would have to make amends with her steward somehow.

But that will have to wait until tomorrow, she thought, wearily.

Logging out to fall asleep on a futon was no longer an option, so Mira would have to sleep here. The only problem was that she'd never slept in-game, so she had no idea where in the Elder's chambers they kept the bedroom.

There has to be one here somewhere, she thought as she began checking the doors in the room.

Behind the first door was the private Collection Room. Many of the rare items she'd gathered from across the world were displayed inside.

The next door opened to reveal her refining room, much to her relief. Just as she remembered, it was filled with all the wisdom and materials that she'd researched as Danblf.

Next was a storeroom filled with weapons, armor, and experimental refined goods filed away in one of Mariana's inscrutable organization schemes.

And behind the fourth door, she found a toilet.

Instantly, Mira realized that she had pressing business that had gone unattended since arriving in this world. Warning signs had been present since just before arriving in Silverhorn, but now she stiffened at the intensifying biological urge rising from her abdomen. It wasn't that she'd forgotten...she'd been feeling the warning signs since just before arriving in Silverhorn. She'd just wanted to forget.

What was it going to be like, doing...*that* while in the form of a young lady? That knowledge, once discovered, could never be forgotten.

But this problem wasn't going away. Rather, it was building and getting worse now that she was confronted with the necessary facility. There was no going back. Mira stepped inside and closed the door to the toilet. Moments later came the soft echo of running water and a sign of relief.

"Luminaria would find this hilarious, no doubt." A bitter smile came to Mira's face as she imagined Luminaria's reaction. She unconsciously put her hand to her belly as she stepped back into the main chamber.

"Well, it was no big deal in the end... The great social equalizer. We all gotta go sooner or later," Mira muttered to herself.

Having now crossed that scandalously unavoidable line, she felt refreshed, and her expression was cheerful. Perhaps there was still the hint of a dirty thought left, but what was she to do? This was her ideal female form, after all, so Mira justified it to herself as pride in a job well done.

High on accomplishment, Mira promptly moved on to the next room, which turned out to be the bath. Filling the tub with hot water, she stripped off her gear and sank into the bath to wash away the sweat and grime of the day's journey.

"This long hair is going to take some getting used to," she said, feeling slightly less drowsy after her bath. Mira set to work with a towel drying her shimmering silver hair.

As she gathered up her clothes, Mira noticed the blood, dirt, and other stains on her robe. She was no germaphobe, but it was filthy, and she couldn't bring herself to put it back on before washing it.

Wrapping the towel around herself to cover her important bits, she sat bare-bottomed on the leather sofa and began sorting through her wardrobe, looking for something that might serve as a dressing gown. One of the items caught her attention: an Angel's Down Raiment.

It had been a special quest reward for completing the Sage's Quest, *Legend of Angels*. While it increased skills exclusive to the Sage class, the design clashed terribly with Danblf's preferred style. Thus, it was consigned to storage, to be forgotten about.

Appearance was everything for Danblf. Regardless of the stats, gear that didn't give the impression of a dignified, stately wizard was never permitted to grace his form. Numbers be damned.

Well, that was then and this is now, thought Mira. The robe was flowing and flawless, and it would probably look pretty good on her. She pulled the Angel's Down Raiment on before she had a chance to change her mind.

It fit her like an oversized babydoll nightie. The hem reached down to her calves and the sleeves midway up her arms, and the light peach-colored fabric was irresistibly soft to the touch. She wasn't entirely sure if it was actually made of angel's down, but it was *heavenly*. It was also clearly not intended for male avatars—no wonder Danblf had been so against it.

"Hrmmm, well, it's not so bad now."

She used the window as a mirror, the darkness of night showing her reflection. Her young body looked amazing in just the robe, and she smiled in admiration and perhaps just a little lust. Then she made a point to comport herself, forcing her expression to settle into one of innocence.

Suitable sleepwear found, she scoured the rest of the chamber to find the bedroom she'd been looking for before getting distracted by hygiene and fashion concerns. While doing so, she stumbled across yet another storage room full of clothing. Pulling out another robe that could be used as a change of clothes, she dumped it on the sofa. Exquisitely decorated and colored, it carried an aura of luxury and had been worn by Danblf for special occasions.

She briefly considered finding a hamper for the laundry before deciding that Mariana would take care of it. Mira left discarded clothes scattered on the floor in Danblf's usual fashion.

Mira let out a small yawn as she leaned against the window, looking down at the streetlights far below. With drooping eyelids, she put her hands on her hips and arched her back in a stretch.

She checked the time in the menu; it was just past 10 p.m., normally the time when the game kicked into high gear. But the long walk through the forest earlier had been fatiguing, and the slight pick-me-up offered by the bath was fleeting. As she gave a second yawn, she rubbed her eyes with the backs of her hands.

According to Lythalia, Luminaria would be back tomorrow. Perhaps there would be answers then.

And so, with nothing else to do but rest and wait, Mira allowed herself to crawl into the bed. The give of the mattress cushioned her little body, and the carefully tucked-in sheets wrapped Mira in Mariana's wishes that someday her master would return.

Nestled near the center of a large crescent-shaped body of water was the aptly named city of Lunatic Lake, capital of Alcait and home of the Royal Palace.

As King Solomon finished with the day's business, he sat back in his wheeled leather chair, pushing his feet off of his paperwork-covered desk. The wheels on the chair gave a light rattle as they carried him to the window. Sitting under lights powered by Ethereal techniques, Solomon touched the silver bracelet hanging on his left arm and stared out into nothing. A window that only he could see popped up before him, filled with a list of names displayed in either gray or white letters.

"Danblf!"

Solomon checked this screen every day. For the first time in three decades, Danblf's name displayed in white.

He looked out into the night where darkness and silence reigned supreme. Just beyond the distant mountains, he could make out the dim lights of the Sacred City of Silverhorn. The city was home to the nation's heroes. Solomon lost himself in fond memories for a moment, and then a soft knock at the door drew him back to the present.

"Come in."

"Sir, I'm sorry to disturb you," said the messenger with a bow. He stepped into the room, a piece of paper grasped in his hand. Solomon nodded impatiently, prompting him to continue, and the messenger unfolded the paper before reading the contents.

"From Captain Graia, First Squadron of the Magic-Clad Knights. He confirms that a pack of monsters appeared near the border. With help from a young female adventurer, the threat was neutralized. However, an unfamiliar creature escaped, and they are currently searching for its whereabouts. There's a postscript— the adventurer is a summoner named Mira. She's described as a lovely young lady with long silver hair."

Solomon listened with a small, unnoticeable frown. Up until this point, the packs of monsters that appeared were composed solely of creatures that lived in the vicinity of Alcait. They should all be well known to the knights charged with ensuring the country's security. For there to be something new out there was troubling.

"Maybe something just got swept along into the horde? Or perhaps... Hmmm." With a sigh, Solomon let the matter rest. As he lifted his head, he saw that the messenger was still standing there with another report clasped in his hands.

"Is there something else?"

"Yessir."

"Very well, go on."

"We received word from Miss Lythalia, attendant of the Tower of Sorcery in Silverhorn, via magical transmission. She has also encountered a girl named Mira, who claims to be the pupil of Master Danblf."

"His...*pupil*?"

Solomon brought the systems screen back up, where the name *Danblf* was marked as online. And now a lady had appeared, claiming to be his pupil, and an unknown adventurer had assisted the knights in destroying a horde of monsters. Both of these mystery women went by the name of Mira.

"This can't be coincidence now, can it?" The exhaustion that had clouded Solomon's eyes after a long day of paperwork was banished by a joyful glow.

"Send someone to Silverhorn right away," he ordered cheerfully. "Tell them to fetch this Mira, but show her the utmost respect! I'll leave the choice of personnel up to you."

"Immediately, sir." Folding the report, the messenger gave a salute before leaving the room. Solomon turned and looked back out the window, back toward the towers of Silverhorn.

The mountains stood pitch black, absorbing any light that touched them, while the lake surrounding the palace glowed as if filled with moonlight.

She
Professed
Herself
Pupil of the
Wise Man

7

THE CHIRPING OF BIRDS announced the coming of the dawn as a horse-drawn carriage raced through Silverhorn, the echo of the hooves thundering through the streets. Flying the coat of arms for the Kingdom of Alcait, it headed straight for the Linked Silver Towers. Anyone up early and on their way to work might wonder what it was doing there.

Sunlight pierced the window above the canopy bed and Mira's consciousness began to slowly surface from slumber. Her thin robe disheveled, she sat up and took a deep breath to jumpstart her foggy mind. Her lingering drowsiness won that round, and she lay back down, blocking her eyes with her forearm.

She began to slip back into the realm of slumber, but just as she drifted away, the quietness of her chambers was disturbed by a muffled sound that repeated itself over and over. The cacophony dragged Mira back to the waking world and her unfocused, blank stare marveled at the unfamiliar luxury of the room surrounding her.

"Where am I...?"

At the sound of her own high-pitched voice, the events of the day before came rushing back. This was accompanied by a dizzying feeling of anxiety and a mumbled "Oh, that's right."

She suppressed a small panic attack.

Sliding her small, unfamiliar body out from under the sheets, she perched on the side of the bed and caught her breath. Her legs peeked out from under her fluttering robes, and the sunlight filtering through the curtains shone across her like a spotlight, emphasizing the pure luster of her skin. She was speechless.

Blushing like a teenager, Mira stared at her skin and gently ran a finger across her thigh. It was soft to the touch. As the electrical signals raced to her brain, she was jolted awake and fully aware that she was still in the same predicament as the day before.

"Who's making such a racket so early in the morning?" Finally awake, she noticed the inexplicable rhythm that had roused her.

Thump, thump, thump—the sound of pounding, followed by distant voices. Mira could make out multiple people talking, and she left the bedroom to find out what was going on. As she neared the front door, her brain finally comprehended the words those voices were saying.

"Miss Mira, are you there? Miss Mira!" came a familiar, elegant female voice.

"Miss Lythalia, are you certain that that Master Danblf's pupil is here?" asked an unfamiliar male voice.

"Of course. She holds the Master Key for the Tower of Evocation, and multiple witnesses saw a silver-haired girl enter the tower last night," the elf's voice answered.

"Could she have gone to an inn afterwards?" the male voice asked.

"If she has the Master Key, why would she stay in an inn?" spoke a second female voice, also familiar. "The tower is fully furnished, and I clean it every day. It's always in perfect order."

So, one man and two women. Mira knew who they were before she opened the door.

"Ah. Hey, Lythalia. Hey, Mariana." Mira rubbed the sleep from her eyes with the back of her hand as she glanced at the two familiar faces.

Then she made eye contact with the other figure, a military man in uniform standing a step behind the two ladies. On his right shoulder hung an armband bearing the symbol of the Kingdom of Alcait.

"And you are—?" he began.

"Miss Mira! What on earth are you wearing?!" cried Lythalia.

"Sir, look away!" commanded Mariana, trying to spin the soldier to face the opposite wall.

Lythalia stood stunned for just a moment before suddenly embracing Mira's almost naked form to shield her from the man's gaze. Mariana was dressed like a maid with hair done up in twin pigtails that shimmered like sapphires. She managed to situate the man so that he no longer had a view of Mira as she spilled out of her sheer robe. Unfortunately, the force of Mariana's action caused him to collide with the opposite wall, and he dropped to the ground with a dull thud.

Meanwhile, Lythalia lifted Mira over her shoulder and carried her back into the bedroom, with Mariana following in their wake and closing the door behind them.

Lythalia dropped Mira unceremoniously onto the leather sofa, and the young woman looked at the elf with a petulant stare.

"What are you two doing?!"

"I believe I should be asking you that. Despite this being the Elder's chambers, you will still sometimes receive visitors. You can't just go prancing to the front door in an outfit that."

Mira looked down to check just what she was wearing to deserve such an admonishment, only to realize that the Angel's Down Raiment was indeed much too revealing. It could hardly be considered underwear, much less clothing.

But Danblf had always dressed down in comfortable clothes when alone in the Elder's chambers—and besides, no other clothing in her inventory fit properly. Even the Wise Man's robes she'd been wearing yesterday were meant for battle, not relaxation. She'd intended to wear them outside but hadn't the slightest intention of wearing them indoors.

"Well, I'm afraid I don't have anything suitable," Mira said indignantly.

"We'll find something for you." Lythalia picked up the red-and-black robe Mira had draped across the sofa the night before and forced it over the young lady's head. "But please, cover yourself up before you get attacked by some lecherous pervert."

Wiggling her way through the robe, Mira popped her head out of the collar only to find that the garment was hopelessly oversized. The hem dragged along the floor and the sleeves flapped far beyond the tips of her fingers. The collar, which was the perfect size for Danblf, was much too wide for Mira. It gaped open in an alluring, suggestive fashion.

"I'm swimming in this."

"Well, it belongs to Master Danblf, so there's little wonder that it doesn't fit," Mariana said with a click of her tongue. She took off one of her hair clips before fastening it to the collar of the robe. The red ribbon-shaped clip pulled the robe tight across Mira's chest and emphasized her figure.

"Oh...oh no, no, no..." Mira's shoulders slumped, as one of her favorite robes lost all of its gravitas with the simple addition of a hair clip.

"Miss Mira, are you truly Master Danblf's pupil?" Mariana asked as she fiddled with Mira's robe. She stared into Mira's eyes, clinging to a thread of hope.

"Indeed, I am. My master has told me much about you, Mariana."

Mariana's naturally sweet disposition compelled others to care about her. She had sapphire-blue hair and eyes, a youthful physique much like Mira's, and gossamer butterfly wings that fluttered on her back. As a fairy, she could rise into the air on gusts of mana, rather than the wind.

"Oh, thank goodness! I-it's just that...j-just that... Oh! Master Danblf..." Tears of relief filled her eyes, spilling over onto her rosy cheeks as if to cool them.

Her unexpected tears caught Mira off guard and she unconsciously reached out toward Mariana. She paused midway and pulled back, rubbing her chin instead. Those tears weren't for her.

They were for Danblf, who had vanished thirty years ago. Guilt gnawed at Mira's stomach.

Should I confess? Perhaps Mariana at least deserves the truth.

But Mira couldn't do it. How could she even begin to explain what had happened? How would the fairy handle the shock that her beloved Danblf was in such a state?

Mira simply didn't know how she'd react. She had known Mariana as an NPC, a computer-driven personality that organized the Elder's chambers, to Danblf's joy and frustration. But now the faithful attendant had agency and a sense of self—a self who felt pain at the loss of her master. Mira was torn between her desire to not be judged for her current state and the need to comfort her assistant and put her worries to rest.

She stared in silence at the sleeves covering her hands, filled with shame as Lythalia gently wiped Mariana's cheeks, offering tender murmurs of "Isn't it wonderful?"

"I'm sorry. I'm better now." As Mariana regained her composure, a familiar rhythm echoed through the room.

"Excuse me, Miss Lythalia? Miss Mariana? Is everything all right?" The military man had come back to his senses and returned to his royal mission.

"Yes, we'll be right with you," Lythalia shouted through the closed door. Then she turned her attention back to her original target, who was currently sprawled on the sofa, playing with the excess length of her sleeves.

"So what does the soldier want?" asked Mira, still nonplussed by the whole situation.

"I reported our meeting yesterday to King Solomon," stated Lythalia matter-of-factly. "Immediately afterward, he sent word that he wanted to meet you at the earliest possible opportunity, Miss Mira. Coming from the king, that means right away. The gentleman outside is the escort he dispatched to bring you to the capital."

"Really? Solomon, you say..."

King Solomon had been a close friend of Danblf and had personally invited him to join his fledgling kingdom. From Mira's perspective, she'd been friends with Solomon even longer than Luminaria.

"Mistress Luminaria is also currently at the capital, so you should be able to speak with her after your audience with the king." Lythalia and Mariana had no knowledge of the long-shared history between the two and yet couldn't help but smile at Mira's blasé attitude toward royalty. From their perspective, Mira spoke with the same mannerisms as Danblf.

"Hrmmm, very well. Then let's be off," Mira said. *If Solomon is here, then he might be a player, just like Luminaria.*

Mira stood from the sofa and made for the exit. But Lythalia and Mariana blocked her from the door.

"Not so fast, Miss Mira."

"Hrmmm, what is it now?"

"Just because you're wearing a robe doesn't mean that you're ready to go." Lythalia was clearly referring to the dragging hem and flopping sleeves. The robe simply didn't fit. "Stand still for a moment and Mariana will have you all fixed up before you know it."

Lythalia's eyes glowed with a suspicious glee, and Mira was captured before she could react. Masses of ribbon were produced from *somewhere* and Mariana set to work fixing the hem and pinning the sleeves, while Lythalia assisted by holding Mira immobile and preventing her from fighting back. Soon enough, she was all dolled up.

"What about underwear?" asked Lythalia, admiring their handiwork.

"That *is* a problem," agreed Mariana.

With the exterior makeover complete, the two remembered the scene of Mira emerging from the chamber wearing naught but the Angel's Down Raiment. This robe might cover everything, but underneath, Mira was still completely naked.

The mere utterance of the word *underwear* caused a chill to run down the Mira's spine. Come to think of it, she didn't have any memories of wearing underwear in the game. Just years and years of Danblf going commando. The only underwear slot item he had was a traditional loincloth handed out during the river festival. There was no way that the two ladies in front of her were going to let this go.

After a moment's thought, Mariana scampered off toward the bathroom that Mira had used the night before. She returned with something clasped in her hand. Mira thought she'd seen it last night but hadn't grasped what it was.

"There we go, this should do it. Now then, Miss Mira."

Mariana's words prompted Lythalia to lift Mira into the air with a quick "By your leave," before Mariana unceremoniously stuffed her into the garment. As she looked down at her new accessory, Mira remembered what they were called. The same frilly underwear she saw on gothic lolita characters.

Drawers.

"But why on earth would I...uh, I mean, why would Master Danblf have *these* in his quarters?" Mira's face glowed red.

She was completely certain that Danblf never had a taste for collecting women's underwear. Had they come home in a pile of loot, unnoticed and filed away by Mariana?

"Well," said Mariana, beginning to blush. "Master Danblf's private quarters are equipped with a large, comfortable bath."

"Yes, it's very nice but..."

"And I keep those here as a spare."

"You... Oh. I see..."

Mira lost the will to resist and nodded her head, submitting to her future as their dress-up doll.

The robe was festooned with countless ribbons, with the hem pulled up and arranged into a facsimile of a flared skirt and the sleeves trussed up before being left to hang loose. Mira looked like she'd been through a magical girl transformation. Lythalia and Mariana nodded in satisfaction, pleased with the fruits of their effort. Mira's expression was frozen into a bitter smile.

"Very well, Miss Mira, shall we see you off?" asked Mariana.

"The envoy is waiting for you," stated Lythalia.

"I can't go out like this."

"It would be rude to make him wait any longer," Lythalia replied.

"I'm not the one who made him wait."

"Well, you couldn't go out looking the way you did," protested Mariana, wringing her hands slightly.

"I'm telling you..." Mira began before she gave up on any hope of winning against the pair. Glancing down at the appearance of her robe, she let out a massive sigh as she realized there was nothing she could do.

"Out we go, then." Lythalia opened the door to reveal the military man, standing upright once again. The only difference was a slight blush on his cheeks.

As Mira left the bedroom, Mariana followed behind and silently closed the door.

The man took in every inch of Mira's ribbon-studded robe, amazed at the change in appearance. A few patches of exposed skin reminded him of the earlier encounter, and he fought to keep that thought from showing on his face.

Not fast enough, unfortunately. Mariana shot him a glare that could kill a dragon. He flinched slightly but rebounded with a light cough before bowing with his right hand clenched to his chest in the royal salute. The sight of it brought back memories for Mira.

That style of salute had been created after the nation had won their first war. Everyone had been giddy over the surprise victory, and in the heat of the moment, the salute was created.

Danblf and the rest, riding high on success and bowing to one another with the clenched fist to their hearts, made for grand nostalgia. Despite the bittersweet memory, she forced a polite smile in response.

"It is a pleasure to make your acquaintance. I am Garrett Astol, vice commander of the Kingdom of Alcait's Mobile Armored Division."

"I'm Mira—" she began before being cut off.

Garrett rolled right over her terse response without even the slightest hesitation. "You must be Mira, Master Danblf's pupil. I come bearing a message from the king."

"We've already explained everything, and Miss Mira has gladly accepted the king's invitation for an audience," Lythalia interjected, looking at Garrett, who was steadfastly trying to avoid making eye contact.

"Oh! Then you have my thanks. Well, there's a carriage waiting for us out front, so let's not delay." With at least a modicum of composure regained, he led Mira to the carriage in a manner that was decidedly not running away from the elf/fairy tag team.

"Take care on your journey!" called Lythalia.

"Miss Mira, perhaps I can ask you more about Master Danblf next time we're together?" asked Mariana.

"Hrmm. I suppose so. Let's talk when next we meet."

"Thank you so much. I'll be looking forward to it!"

CHAPTER 7

"Indeed. Very well, then."

With a small wave, Mira clambered aboard the carriage, already brainstorming on a better cover story for their next encounter.

She Professed Herself Pupil of the Wise Man

THE PAVED ROAD between Silverhorn and Lunatic Lake passed through a dense forest where the trees echoed with the sound of pounding hooves.

Decorated with a Pegasus motif and pulled by two thoroughbred horses, the carriage raced along its route. This was one of the kingdom's fast courier coaches, only used to ferry VIPs in times of urgency. Having this vehicle dispatched to collect Mira meant that King Solomon desperately wanted to meet her.

As the carriage swayed, Mira stared out the window at the scenery flying past and marveled at the speed. In the game world, she'd use her Floating Island when traveling long distances, but she hadn't been able to find that option in her game menu. After pondering that for a bit, she reached the conclusion that even if the option were still present, Floating Islands might not work as intended—or even at all!—in this new reality.

The coach ride was pleasant enough, she decided. It gave her time to simply relax and enjoy the new normal. The puzzles and mysteries of this new world could wait.

But two hours after they'd left Silverhorn, Mira was beginning to get a little fidgety. She found herself facing the same biological predicament that had troubled her the night before. But this time, the vibration of the carriage conspired with her bladder to speed the situation to a crisis point. With no other option available, she leaned out to have a word with Vice Commander Garrett.

"Say, would you know of a privy nearby?" she shouted into the rush of the oncoming wind.

"Eh? If you're looking for privacy out here, the interior of the carriage should do. But we are almost at Silverwand and we might be able to find a private room there."

"No, I don't need *privacy*. I...I need to see a man about a horse."

"Are the horses not to your standards, miss? I suppose they could use a break, as could I. We're running a bit late, but we'll be in Silverwand soon enough."

"N-no. No! A privy! I need a powder room!"

"I...I'm sorry, I don't know if we'll find that in Silverwand. And don't you think you're a bit young to be playing with gunpowd—"

"Seriously?! A toilet! A bathroom! A pisser! Ugh! Forget it, here is fine. Just pull over and I'll find a tree!" Mira shouted, repeatedly poking Garrett in the back and pointing at an appropriate spot in out in the woods.

"Huh? Ah...oh!! Of course!"

Danblf would no doubt have been able to hold it. Unfortunately, the new form had a smaller capacity, and Mira could feel that she was fast reaching the overflow limit. If she didn't do something soon, she might spring a leak.

The horses slowed down to a walk, but Mira had no time to lose. Leaping from the still-rolling carriage, she rushed behind a tree and pulled up the hem of her robe only to encounter a riddle. The drawers covering her lower half had not come with an instruction manual. Her hands paused, but her legs refused to stop moving—thighs tucked inward as her feet restlessly stamped at the ground.

How the hell do I get these off?!

The drawers threatened to turn an emergency into a tragedy. There wasn't an elastic band, and when she tried to force them down, she found that her hips thwarted her efforts. In a moment of panic, she wondered if she could simply tear them away. Then she remembered that they were borrowed.

That presented a terrible dilemma. What would be worse: destroying borrowed underpants, or leaking into them?

Trying as hard as she could, Mira pulled at the waist, trying to stretch it sideways.

No luck there either! With sweat gushing out of every pore, she looked down at where her fingers were clutching the waistband and gave a strained laugh.

Buried in the frilly lace at the waistline was a ribbon keeping the whole thing bound together. If only she'd kept her cool, she would have seen it immediately. But perhaps missing it was understandable given the huge number of firsts that she'd been asked to deal with over the past twenty-four hours.

String untied, drawers at her knees, Mira squatted. Sweet relief followed.

Having successfully taken care of this problem for the second time, Mira was certain that she had a handle on the basic function and operation of her new body. Her newfound sense of mastery lasted only a few brief seconds. Just as she was about to stand up and re-situate her drawers, she remembered that ladies had to wipe.

"But what am I going to use?" She didn't have any paper on hand. Her Item Box was no help either—she found nothing but food, refining tools, and a few metal items. Closing the menu, Mira looked about for anything close by that might serve as a substitute.

Sunlight filtered down through the treetop canopy and she could hear the soft cries of the forest creatures. Wildflowers peeked out through gaps in the undergrowth.

Staring out at the natural beauty that surrounded her, Mira chose a large white flower with a muttered apology. Squatting again, she did what had to be done.

"Sorry to make you wait." Mira's voice rang out from behind Garrett where he'd been happily brushing down the two horses.

"Think nothing of it, miss. My apologies for the misunderstanding." Garrett turned to her, looking very serious as he bowed deeply.

"Don't let it trouble you. I should have been clearer."

Mira's joy at getting a handle on her new body reflected on her face. Though he was perplexed by her happiness, Garrett felt his tension abate as he opened the carriage door for her.

"Just a bit further and we can stop in Silverwand. We'll find ourselves some breakfast there."

"Very well, drive on." Mira climbed into the carriage as Garrett checked the harnesses of the two horses and then jumped onto the coachman's seat.

Nearly an hour later, the horses were still going strong and the carriage was nearing Silverwand. Alas, Mira faced an unimaginable hardship.

What on earth is this stinging?! Mira writhed in agony on the seat of the carriage. A burning pain had taken up residence in her nethers, the likes of which she'd never felt before.

At first she'd worried it might be a feminine issue because of the location of the problem. But the pain kept growing. Reaching her breaking point, she stripped off her drawers in the privacy of the coach to check the nature of the discomfort. There she found the cause.

"It looks like poison ivy..."

It must have been the flower. It was the only culprit Mira could put her finger on. This certainly didn't conform to any feminine biological imperative—at least none that she was aware of.

With the cause determined, she opened her Item Box and looked for something that might help. She took out one of the standard restorative items she always kept on hand, a Cure-All Salve that removed abnormal conditions and cured light wounds.

Fighting her own reluctance, Mira curled up in the corner of the carriage seat and applied the ointment to the affected area while doing her best to think happy thoughts.

Soon enough, her hypothesis proved correct. The antidote neutralized the flower's rash. Relieved, Mira flopped over in her seat, muttering, "Never again ..."

Ten minutes after the petal affair came to a satisfying conclusion, the carriage came to a gentle stop and Garrett peeked in from his perch.

"Miss Mira, we've arrived in Silverwand. Shall we head to a restaurant? Or would you perhaps like me to get something for you?"

She would have immediately asked for the latter back on Earth, but up until this point, she'd lived in a world where VR was sufficient for most things. Mira thought for a moment before reaching her decision. "I could stretch my legs. Let's head to the restaurant."

She was in a different world now. Walking through the forest, face-to-face interactions with people, riding in the carriage. While seemingly inconvenient compared to the life she'd left behind, Mira was genuinely starting to take pleasure in these experiences.

She stepped away from the carriage to stare up at the blue sky.

Silverwand was home to people who made a living via farming, forestry, and mining. Located in a valley of the mountain range that separated Lunatic Lake from Silverhorn, it also served as the waystation between the kingdom's political and magical capitals. The young city was prospering as a trading hub.

They were currently in one of the parking areas near the city's commercial district. It was a grassy field bordered by several stables offering coach services to nearby towns. Since the royal coach occupied one of the national stables, there was no charge for the stop. Only the king, aristocrats, and VIP carriages had that privilege, and that drew the attention of everyone in the vicinity.

Attention was focused on a young woman of uncommon beauty. Her appearance—white skin, lustrous silver hair, sparkling eyes, and ribbon-laden robe—left them speechless.

Mira stared up at the surrounding mountain skyline while stretching to remove the kinks from her muscles. A bird caught her attention, and she tracked it across the sky before shifting her attention to other birds taking flight here and there across the forest. She slowly spun around, taking it all in with no sense of self-awareness.

The faint sound of Garrett working his way through some horse-related chores washed over her, and she lowered her gaze to find the surrounding townsfolk looking in her direction. She quickly faced the side of the coach to avoid eye contact.

"They're staring at my ridiculous outfit. Damn that elf and fairy..." she muttered.

She looked like she'd come straight out of an anime. There was no way her absurd outfit blended into this fantasy world. But just as Mira was about to sprint for the hills, Garrett finished his tasks and wandered back over to her side.

"I appreciate your patience. Now, what would you like to eat, Miss Mira?"

"Whatever you recommend," Mira responded, using Garrett's body to shield herself from the crowd.

"I know just the place. Follow me."

She prodded his back in an attempt to hurry him away from the staring townsfolk. The sight of the impatient girl pestering the soldier only charmed them even further.

Leaving the parking lot, Mira and Garrett turned off the main street and soon found themselves in front of a tavern with an attached inn.

"Here we are. It may be small, but the food here is to die for!"

Mira looked at the wooden building. The sign above a set of saloon doors proclaimed it The Twilight Crossing. She'd seen doors like those before in westerns. Normally, they offered a view of the tavern's interior—but due to Mira's short stature, all she could see was the ceiling.

"You don't come around for ages, and when you do, the first thing you do is call us small. How rude!" They turned to see a woman standing there, staring at Garrett.

She was in her mid-twenties and carried a shopping basket in either hand. Simple and beautiful, her chestnut hair flowed from under a bandana to drape over her shoulder. Her white-and-blue apron was emblazoned with the words *The Twilight Crossing*, taking all the mystery out of her place of employment.

"Hi, Cherie. Long time no see."

"You're telling me. You should think about visiting more often... Wait. Who is this adorable girl?!" Catching sight of Mira peeking out from behind Garrett, Cherie dropped one of the shopping baskets and instinctively lunged to pat her on the head.

"Whoa! Hands off!" Mira brushed Cherie's hand away and moved to keep Garrett between herself and the woman.

"She's so cute!"

"This is Miss Mira," Garrett said, ears reddening as he observed Cherie's maternal instinct kick into high gear.

"Oh, Mira, is it? What a lovely little name for a lovely little girl. *Mira*." Cherie said the name as if she was trying it on for size. Her expression kept getting softer as she sidled closer and closer to Mira.

"Cherie, best keep your distance," Garrett admonished. "Miss Mira doesn't seem to be enjoying this."

"Darn right!" piped Mira from Garrett's shadow.

"So tell me, Garrett. What are you doing with little Mira here?" Cherie asked after taking a moment to restrain herself.

"I'm escorting her to Lunatic Lake. We're just making a quick stop for breakfast."

"So that's why you're here." Cherie picked up her shopping basket and swung the door open, ushering them both inside. "All right, there're some open spots at the counter, go ahead and wait there... Aw, are you still mad at me, Mira?"

Cherie seemed crestfallen and stared at Mira, who was still on her guard and tucked up against Garrett.

"I don't think Miss Mira is the type to hold a grudge," Garrett said while situating himself on a stool.

He was right...sort of. She wasn't exactly angry, just terribly embarrassed. But she also didn't want to hurt the woman's feelings, so she stepped out from behind the soldier.

"Just don't treat me like a kid."

Not a large request. But to Cherie, it made her seem even more like a little girl trying her hardest to act like an adult. She had an overwhelming urge to smother her with affection.

"You're just too cute!" And with that she tossed her baskets to the side and leapt at Mira, catching her in a tight embrace. Realizing the honest affection and the impossibility of escape, Mira gave in with a sigh.

"Fine. Just...get it out of your system."

She Professed Herself Pupil of the Wise Man

AFTER FINISHING UP breakfast at The Twilight Crossing, Mira sipped on a berry au lait that Cherie had given her. The drink was the perfect blend of tart and sweet, and Mira's expression relaxed as she enjoyed it. Cherie was delighted to watch and dote on the girl at every opportunity.

Had Mira gotten used to it? Or had she just given in? Even she didn't know for sure. Either way, she was no longer rebuffing Cherie's coddling.

Garrett smiled at the two of them from where he was chatting with Valga, the innkeeper and Cherie's father. Valga had short-cropped hair, the same chestnut brown as Cherie's, and a physique tempered by life in the mountains. Although he was a gruff-looking fellow, he was known for cooking incredibly delicate cuisine.

The traveling pair had enjoyed sandwiches for breakfast—roast chicken and vegetables on white bread. That was followed up by a complimentary custard tart that Cherie brought out for Mira. Both had been made by Valga, who was just as fastidious about his food's appearance as he was with its flavor.

"So when are you going to propose to my daughter?" joked Valga with a smile that indicated he wasn't really joking.

Garrett could only muster a weak grin in response—this was the reason he didn't come around the tavern much anymore. He didn't have the courage to say that his appetite had outweighed his embarrassment this morning.

Noticing that Mira had finished her berry au lait, he drained his tea in a single gulp and rose to his feet. "Well, I think it's time for us to be on our way."

"Aw, come on. Stay a bit longer," pouted Cherie, taking her eyes off Mira for the first time since she entered the shop.

"I'm afraid I can't. King's business, after all," Garrett replied as he took out his wallet and placed exact change on the counter.

"Indeed. Time we were off." Mira took advantage of Cherie's distraction to slip out from under her arm. As she watched her go with a sad expression in her eyes Cherie began to tidy away the counter.

"Not you too, Mira!" As she watched her go with a sad look in her eyes, Cherie began to tidy up the counter.

"Thank you for the meal. I'll see you next time," Garrett said.

Mira mumbled a half-hearted thanks of her own.

"Come back whenever," Valga said with a slight smile. "That goes for the both of you. I'll have another one of those berry au laits waiting for you, miss."

Despite being focused on resettling her ribbon-covered mess of a robe, Mira couldn't help but react to the words "berry au lait." After a moment's thought, Mira settled on a suitable compromise.

"Hrmmm, perhaps I'll stop in when your daughter's not around."

"Mira! You meanie!"

"Best check in just before noon, then. That's usually when she's out shopping," Valga replied.

"Ho ho! I'll make sure to remember that."

"Don't encourage her, Father!" Cherie leaned against the counter, overcome as she realized they were conspiring against her.

After leaving The Twilight Crossing, the pair returned to the parking area and Mira rushed to board to the carriage before garnering any further attention. The two horses had been well attended by the caretaker and were in high spirits. Whinnying as their harnesses were reattached, they showed no sign of fatigue.

Mira looked out of the window as the carriage began to drive away, observing the streets of Silverwand with interest. It was so... *new*. The freshness of the town rushing by the window stirred a feeling of hopefulness within her.

The carriage followed the main road through the city before rejoining the forest highway. Following that route into the hills led to a cliff towering before them. The hillside had been reinforced with stone blocks, and the road led into a tunnel beneath the mountains.

Mira was quite surprised as the interior of the coach suddenly darkened. She looked out the back window and saw the tunnel's entrance growing smaller as the carriage rushed along. This was another new piece of construction. She didn't remember there being any tunnels in the mountain that separated Lunatic Lake and Silverhorn during her time in the game.

She shouted up to Garrett, "This tunnel is quite amazing. When was it built?"

"Benedict Tunnel? Let me think. I'm fairly sure construction began thirty years ago under orders from King Solomon. It took about five years to complete."

"Ho ho. You don't say," she replied. Looking ahead, Mira saw the tunnel was lit by Ethereal lights spaced evenly along the walls, and she chuckled at how predictably Solomon-esque that design feature was.

The mountain range that separated Lunatic Lake and Silverhorn had once made it very inconvenient to travel between the two locations. If Floating Islands weren't in use and the main mode of transportation was horse-drawn carriage, then this tunnel would be an essential public road.

Mira also gleaned another tidbit of interesting information from Garrett's explanation—Solomon had ordered the tunnel to be built thirty years ago. That meant Solomon had been in this world for the full thirty years she had been absent.

Now she just needed to confirm this was the same Solomon she knew as a player.

Thanks to this tunnel and the rapid speed of the coach, they would arrive at the capital to meet the king fairly soon. Mira returned to her seat and continued to peer out the window.

The echo of the horseshoes, the monotony of the tunnel, the satisfaction of a good meal, and the coach's cradle-like rocking worked a sort of magic. Unable to resist such an enchanting combination, Mira's head lolled to her chest and she began to snore softly.

Blue sky stretched out overhead, reflected in the calm waters of a crescent-shaped lake.

Near the center of the lake's inner crescent sat the Royal Palace, home of Solomon, King of Alcait. The rest of the lakeside was surrounded by the capital city.

The carriage exited the tunnel and began descending the mountain. Passing through the lightly forested foothills, it made its way across the pale and dusky Rugged Plateau. The plateau was a jumble of plants and rocks. Small animals peeked their heads out of holes and burrows to watch the passing coach with curiosity.

A sudden beam of sunlight pierced the carriage and woke Mira from her slumber. She rubbed her eyes and moved to the other side of the seat to escape the blinding light. With a yawn, she perched her arm on the windowsill and rested her chin on her hand. The breeze coming in through the window fluttered through her silver hair and cooled her body, still warm from her impromptu nap. Watching the scenery drift by, she quenched her thirst with a bottle of apple au lait.

"Ho ho. Looks like the capital has grown as well!" Mira mused as she looked out ahead at the large cityscape.

From her vantage point on the Rugged Plateau, she could see a large circle of imposing ramparts that surrounded the city and turned the crescent lake into a full moon. The city was much larger than she remembered.

One unfamiliar structure stood out, so she stuck her head out of the window to ask Garrett about it.

"Say, what's that large building?" Mira asked, pointing in the general direction.

"Which one?" Garrett glanced at her happy expression and tried to follow her excitedly bouncing finger.

The obvious "that large building" would be the palace in the center of the city, but Garrett was sure that Mira knew that already. That left four other buildings she might be referring to—a series of colossal structures arrayed at the four cardinal directions, halfway between the palace and the city walls.

"Oh, you mean the Five Elements."

"The Five Elements?"

"Yes, they were built during the same period as the Benedict Tunnel and were based on a city development proposal by King Solomon. That one to the south of the palace is the Waste Treatment Plant, followed by the Alcait Academy there in the east, then the Drug Research Institute up north, and finally, the Artisans Workshop Bureau in the west. Collectively, they're all called the Five Elements."

The five elements of wood, fire, earth, metal, and water stemmed from Chinese cosmological teachings and were seen in practices such as *feng shui*. They were also seen in the design of cities like Kyoto. Mira was certain that that was where Solomon had gotten the idea for this city development plan.

"Ho ho. I see," she said. *Sort of, anyway. I count four buildings, but I suppose the palace would be the fifth.*

During their time in the game, Solomon's love for *feng shui* developed into a burning passion. Every time Danblf saw him, he'd give tips and tricks to increase luck in finance or business.

With her curiosity abated, Mira went back to her seat and put her arm back on the windowsill. Sipping at her apple au lait, she watched a flock of migratory birds join a larger flock flying their way across the sky. She couldn't help but feel happy.

Putting the now-empty bottle of apple au lait on the floor of the carriage near her feet, she pulled two more from her inventory before offering one to Garrett.

"How about a drink?"

"Why, thank you, Miss Mira." He happily grasped the bottle.

"So why'd you join the army?" Mira asked, fishing for a topic.

"Why I joined up?" Garrett muttered to himself, then took a sip of his drink while thinking of his answer. He paused to appreciate the beverage. "This is delicious."

"Isn't it?" she said with a smile.

"I suppose I joined up because of my father."

"Oh? Your father's also in the military?"

"He is. It's a bit embarrassing to admit, but I've always admired him. He's the captain of the First Squadron of the Magic-Clad Knights, and I grew up wanting to be just like him." Garrett's eyes gently shone with admiration as he spoke.

"You're a good son. I'm sure your father would be proud to hear you say that."

"Oh, no, I could never actually tell him this face to face. You can't tell anyone I said this, Miss Mira."

He mimed shushing her, finger to his lips, but his expression belied the depths of his feelings. While the gesture was what one would normally do to admonish a child, Mira was willing to forgive it—just this once.

"Your father's a lucky man." Mira slightly envied his father. Any dad would be lucky to have a son who thought so highly of them.

"You think so?"

"Of course. If I'm ever a father, I'd hope to have a dutiful son like yourself."

"Well, in your case Miss Mira, I believe you'd be a mother, right?"

"Ah. I-I suppose so..."

She stammered for a moment at Garrett's reminder before giving a wry smile. A mother instead of a father. She hadn't thought about it at all, but if she became a parent, that was how it would be.

She *did* want children...someday. Kagami had thought about what it would be like to have kids, what he'd name them, and what they'd play together. But those memories were in the distant past, part of another life.

Maybe she didn't have to be a parent to watch over and guide children. *Maybe some other role would be all right*, she thought. But that was a matter for the future. For the moment, she could just enjoy a second life in a new body. With that, she sipped her second bottle of apple au lait.

She Professed Herself Pupil of the Wise Man

THE CARRIAGE GRADUALLY SLOWED before coming to a stop before a large, imposing gate.

"Look how they've grown!" exclaimed Mira as she leaned from the carriage, thrilled by the difference between what stood before her and what she remembered from thirty years prior. From the plateau looking out over the city, the city walls looked like a thin circle surrounding the capital, but up close, they perfectly embodied the spirit of the Kingdom of Alcait and its strong focus on national defense.

If the walls had changed this much, how different was the city within them? What sort of new and wonderful changes awaited her discovery?

The coach did not bring her to the main city gates. Instead, it approached a private entrance that opened to a boulevard leading directly to the palace.

Garrett exchanged a few words with the sentry, and soon, the large gate opened with a dull, heavy thud. The guard signaled with his hand and a bell atop it began to ring. It was answered by another bell far in the distance, and peals announced the arrival of the Pegasus Carriage for all to hear.

Traffic was stopped to give the coach the right of way. There were five intersections along the avenue, all of which were temporarily blocked by guards using black-and-yellow batons to halt other passersby.

"Well, now, isn't this quite the welcome," muttered Mira to herself.

Leaning out of the carriage, she could see a line of evenly spaced sentries, stretching from the open gate down the street to the palace. The carriage started off again, gradually increasing its speed. It reached a sprint only a few seconds later, and the city scenery flew by at a dizzying pace.

Locals watched the coach race past with curiosity. When they saw that Garrett was the coachman, their interest only grew. They knew that this must be a serious situation indeed.

Mira began to pick out details in the blur of scenery rushing past her window. One building in particular caught her attention; it was the Artisans Workshop Bureau, one of the Five Elements. Reminiscent of classic German architecture, the sight caused Mira to immediately add a tour of the Five Elements to her sightseeing wish list.

Up close like this, you really get a feel for the size of it.

After a short while, the carriage slowed, stopping at the gate before the royal palace. Mira stretched to remove the stiffness of the long journey and then stealthily added the empty apple au lait bottle to its partners on the floor near her feet.

"We've arrived at our destination, Miss Mira." Opening the door of the carriage, Garrett bowed and extended a hand to help her down from the coach.

"Well done," Mira said. Then she slapped his hand with an added "Get that away."

She jumped from the carriage. Glancing at the palace, she noted with a sigh of half relief and half disappointment that at least this was still the same as she remembered.

Then she was immediately at a loss for words.

Behind the slowly opening gates, an even more grandiose welcome than they'd received on the main road was presenting itself. On both sides of the path to the palace doors, a line of motionless knights stood with their swords held in a position of salute. Behind them were more knights holding spears. Mixed in at regular intervals were soldiers bearing the national flag.

"Isn't this all...a bit much?"

"It just goes to show how pleased King Solomon is to meet you, Miss Mira."

"Of course," muttered Mira with a sigh.

"Master Danblf is one of our national heroes, after all. It's the least we can do when his pupil comes calling."

"Hrmmm. Is that so?"

"It is indeed. Now then, Miss Mira, shall we continue?"

As they stepped away from the carriage, a castle caretaker stepped forward to lead the horses to the stables.

The moment Mira and Garrett stepped through the gates, her eardrums were assaulted with the loud, rhythmic pounding of drums. The knights raised their weapons, creating an arched tunnel of arms for the vice commander and magical girl to pass under on their walk to the palace entrance.

"Surely this is...just too much."

"I don't know, I kind of like it," shouted Garrett to be heard over the noise. He seemed to be enjoying himself.

Well, that's very forward for an official escort, Mira grumped, but in truth, she found his carefree personality charming and made a note of mental praise. Solomon still chose his subordinates well, it seemed.

The two passed through the extravagant archway to the palace with the sounds of drums and fifes ringing behind them. The guards stationed at the entrance to the palace bowed, opening the passageway to the throne room. Mira entered, grateful to be somewhere quieter with less pomp and circumstance.

Inside the throne room, the elegant scent of flowers wafted through the air. The floor was covered with different colored squares of carpet, spreading out before Mira in an evenly spaced pattern of black, blue, green, red, and white.

Five people were already present in the throne room, but the most conspicuous was the boy sitting on the throne itself.

A crown adorned with countless jewels sat atop his head, and his light-green hair just slightly covered his golden eyes. At first glance, he seemed out of place, but Mira had no doubt that the boy dressed in opulent garb and sitting upon the throne was in fact the king. His subjects knew that his thirty-year reign of prosperity was a testament to his wisdom.

King Solomon of Alcait stared down at Mira with a mischie-vous grin on his face. He looked exactly as Mira remembered, though perhaps his clothing was slightly more ostentatious than before. At the foot of the dais stood a knight who exuded a superhuman aura, and a mage wearing a black robe and hood. The mage glanced at Mira and offered a soft smile, but the knight sighed in bitter disappointment.

Garrett stepped forward and knelt. "Your Majesty, may I present the pupil of Elder Danblf, the Lady Mira."

"You've done well on this journey, Vice Commander. You may stand down," replied the man standing next to the king in formal tones. Mira recognized him as Solomon's attendant, Suleiman. He was a handsome elf with long blond hair.

Garrett excused himself and stepped off to the side.

"A pleasure to meet you, Miss Mira. I am Suleiman, attendant to the king."

"So I've heard. And I'm Mira."

She shifted just her gaze to Suleiman as she gave her succinct reply, causing Garrett to tense up at her casual tone.

Oblivious to Garrett's mounting panic, Mira simply crossed her arms and put a hand to her chin as she attempted to use the Inspection command on Solomon. No information came floating into view. Glancing back over at Suleiman, she instantly got a full report.

Something's fishy here...

"I apologize for the rudeness, but we would like to confirm

your status as the pupil of Master Danblf. Is this acceptable?" Suleiman asked, interrupting Mira's thought.

"Sure, fine by me." Pulling her Master Key from her Item Box, she began walking toward Suleiman. "Here you go."

It was a short trip. As she approached the dais, the knight leapt forward with a drawn sword.

"Step no closer! You've got some nerve!" he bellowed, pointing his sword at Mira.

According to her Inspection, this was Reynard, knight commander of the King's Guard.

He had been warned by Solomon prior to the audience that the coming guest would probably not show proper deference and that he was not to overreact. He endured her lack of kneeling. He seethed at her language. But this—trying to approach the king without permission—was too much!

"But how else would I show my evidence?" Mira asked. There were some new customs at court, and she disliked the changes. Solomon and Danblf had long been equals, and as far as Mira was concerned, she was only here to see a friend. She had been so caught up in the chance to have a chat that she'd forgot that she was technically having an audience with the ruling power of the country.

"You should have presented it to the guard in attendance!"

"What a bother."

The anger on the knight's face intensified. Unaware of the proper formalities for such a situation, she pinched the end of

Reynard's sword between her fingers before presenting her Master Key to the knight.

"Very well, then. My mistake. Go on and deliver this for me."

"How *dare* you?! Remove yourself at once!"

Enraged, Reynard put all his strength into drawing back his sword, but it refused to budge from where it was held between Mira's fingers. He gaped in astonishment.

"Reynard, bring it here, please," the boy's voice called from the throne.

"But King Solomon...her insolence!"

"I told you that she would be an exception. Do you intend to waste more of my time?"

The knight quailed under the Solomon's glare. But from the way he snatched the Master Key from her, Mira wondered for a moment if she'd made a mistake. Eh, it didn't matter.

Mira released the tip of the sword. Reynard glared at her thin, white arms from where they peeked out of her robe, concluding that she must have used some suspicious and possibly forbidden technique. He'd be more vigilant against her tricks in the future.

Meanwhile, Garrett breathed a sigh of relief that the situation seemed to have settled itself without devolving into violence.

As Mira returned to her previous position, Reynard presented the Master Key to Solomon.

"This is undoubtedly the property of Danblf. And if you claim he passed it to you as a master to a pupil, we have no reason to doubt you."

With that settled, Solomon passed the Master Key to the

Reynard, who returned it to Mira in turn. As Mira placed her Master Key back in her Item Box, she allowed her gaze to wander so as to avoid Reynard's piercing glare.

"And with that taken care of, why don't we change the venue? As you're the pupil of Danblf, I'd be very interested in hearing what your master has been up to for the past thirty years. Agreed?"

"Fine by me," she said. Thinking silently to herself, *Anything to get out of here.*

"Very well, shall we move to my office? It should be a bit more peaceful. The rest of you can join the festivities on the parade grounds."

"King Solomon. Even if she is the pupil of Master Danblf, we don't really know who she is. It's dangerous to be alone with her. Please, allow me to accompany you!" the knight pleaded, casting a sharp glance toward Mira before bowing deeply to his king.

This is just getting tedious. Mira shook her head with exasperation.

"Reynard, are you saying that you believe this girl could best *me*?" Solomon questioned Reynard with unusual emphasis.

While he might have looked like a young boy, there was a reason Solomon had ruled the kingdom for thirty years. In *AEO*, simple politics were not enough—the future of a nation depended on its leader's valor and skill in battle.

"N-no, Your Majesty. But this girl, she uses strange magic. We must be on guard."

Mira had no clue what Reynard meant by strange magic, or what his problem was in general. She speculated it was that he, a big strong man, felt he could not *possibly* have lost a test of strength to her, a waif of a girl. Of course, he didn't know that she had huge stat boosts from her equipment, and she didn't feel like clarifying at the moment.

"Mira...are you planning on causing me harm?"

"Why would I want to do that? I'm just here for a chat."

At Mira's response, a smile fluttered across Solomon's face. "There. You see? And I would like to chat with her as well. So please, Reynard, be reasonable."

"But sir, if anything were to happen to you I would..." Reynard's hands were clenched into fists.

"How about this?" the black-hooded mage interrupted. "Sir Reynard and I will wait in the hallway outside of the office. If anything happens, we will be able to immediately respond. Not even Master Danblf himself, much less Lady Mira, could do something to the king in that short a time. Agreed?"

"Hm, well...I suppose," grumbled the knight.

"Then it's settled. I was looking forward to the party, but if you refuse to budge, then I have no choice but to join you. Reynard and myself—that should be enough, don't you think?" The mage beamed as he clapped a hand to Reynard's shoulder.

"A splendid idea. I apologize, Joachim. We'll hold another party sometime soon." Solomon gave a deep nod before rising to his feet a moment later.

"Oh, no, that's not necessary, Your Majesty. I'll just have Sir Reynard here treat me to something later."

"Rrrgh..." Reynard growled with a pained expression.

CHAPTER 10

"Now then, shall we?" Solomon led the three down the corridor to his office.

**She
Professed
Herself
Pupil** of
the
Wise Man

11

MIRA AND SOLOMON were alone inside the king's office, an impressive mess of a room with a spectacular view of the lake. Reynard and Joachim waited in the corridor, just outside the door.

Bookshelves lined the wall of the fifth-floor office, containing tomes of history, techniques, and literature gathered from around the world. Solomon sat back heavily in his leather chair in the middle of it all. Mira cleared off some of the documents that had been piled high on the sofa before tucking herself into the cramped corner and glancing around the room.

"Quite the mess you have here."

"That's what happens when you've got too much work and not enough time to do it." With the door closed, Solomon's public speech pattern gave way to a casual cadence. "Phew, it's just nice to get a chance to relax and talk to someone."

"Yeah, I bet."

Pleasantries settled, the pair both sat up and exchanged looks.

"Before anything else, I just want to get this straight, right?" said Solomon, holding up his index finger as he fixed Mira with an intense stare.

"Hrmmm? And what's that?" Mira asked, half focused on Solomon and half on moving more paperwork to the floor so she had more room to sit.

"You're Danblf. Am I right?"

A folder fell and scattered paper across the floor as Mira turned to stare at Solomon, her eyes tinged with astonishment. There had been no probing questions. Nor had there been a chance for her to spin her cover story. She'd been trying to come up with a way to delicately broach the subject, hopefully in a way that she could save a little face. She never thought that Solomon would just drop the bombshell out of nowhere.

His mischievous countenance shifted into a beaming smile, as if that was all the confirmation he needed. And that expression confirmed to Mira that this was the Solomon she remembered. This was the boy that was her best friend and greatest rival, the king at whose side she'd fought at so long ago.

She didn't know how he knew, but at least this took care of the elephant in the room. Leaving the fallen documents where they were, she turned and sank back into the sofa. Now maybe she could get some straight answers about what was going on in this world—without the song-and-dance routine.

"Good game." Mira needed to say nothing else.

Solomon smirked.

"Just look at you! You look completely different!" he chortled, trying to hide it with his hands. Every time he glanced over at Mira, the giggles started up again.

"Yeah, well...this change was made with *great* care and consideration, I'll have you know." Mira pouted and glared at Solomon, her face locked in a sullen scowl.

"It's just such a huge change! But hey, the cute girl look *really* suits you."

"Quiet, you."

Suppressing his giggles, Solomon gave Mira another once-over before giving her a nod as his seal of approval. Mira pursed her lips and pointedly looked away. No one watching the exchange would ever imagine this was a meeting between the leader of a nation and that nation's most powerful wizard.

"So long as we're asking questions, let me ask you something." Mira jumped straight at the most important question. "What's going on with this world?"

Finished with his laughing fit, Solomon regained his composure and thought for a moment. Then he gave a clear, concise answer.

"I don't know."

"You don't know?" Mira's eyes slightly widened at Solomon's response. "You've been here for thirty years, and you still don't have the slightest idea?"

"Nope. All I know is that this world is real, and it's not the game anymore. But is it somewhere within our universe? Or are we totally off the grid? Perhaps it's something else that we can't even begin to understand. I don't have those answers."

"I see. But do we know this world is real, at the very least?"

"I'm pretty certain about that. I've never heard of a hallucination that was clear and consistent for over thirty years." Solomon shrugged and looked over at an area of his bookshelves that contained dozens of volumes of detailed historical records from the last thirty years. Gathering that many had been quite a feat, and he nodded to himself in satisfaction.

"Well...to *me*, this could all still be just a dream."

"That line only works because you've been here for two days. Too bad, it's real!"

Two days. Yesterday and today. That reminded Mira of another question.

"By the way, how on earth did you know that I was actually Danblf?"

She'd been trying to give as few hints as possible. The Master Key was kind of a giveaway, but the cover that it had been given to her by her master was a good one. It had certainly fooled Lythalia and Mariana. And the chance that Danblf would come stumbling back to civilization thirty years later was incredibly low. But somehow Solomon knew she was Danblf immediately, and Mira wanted to know what her tell was.

"Hmmm, well. Long story short, I received a report from the Magic-Clad Knights about an encounter with a young girl named Mira, a summoner with an insanely powerful Dark Knight. Then there was another report that a young girl named Mira appeared in the Tower of Sorcery claiming to be Danblf's pupil."

"That's all it took to tip you off?"

"Oh, no! Those reports came in last night just after I checked my Friends List. I saw your name had switched to online."

"Wait, Friends List?" Mira knew what a Friends List was, but her confusion stemmed from where to find one on the game menu.

If she'd seen it in one of the menus, she probably would have already checked it herself. But she hadn't because the Friends List was part of the systems menu, which had disappeared. But did that mean Solomon had access to menus that she didn't?

"The systems menu is gone. How did you check it?"

"Oh, right. If you just got here yesterday, you'd only know how we used to do it in-game."

Solomon put his fingers to the bracelet on his left arm to open the menu and kept poking away, paging between screens that only he could see.

"You have to do it like this. Give it a try." He walked her through what he was pressing, since neither could see each other's screen.

"Ho ho... This will be useful." She saw options for *Friends List*, *Map*, and *Blessings*. "This option is new."

She tapped the map option floating before her. The window went black and nothing happened. Fiddling with it didn't seem to work, so she thought she might get a faster answer by asking. "What's with the map option? I don't remember this."

"It's a new function," said Solomon, dismissing his own interface. "If you drop a map into the *Special Items* category of your Item Box, you'll be able to bring it up with the *Map* option. It's pretty convenient."

"Ho ho. Indeed." Mira instantly understood just how useful the feature would be.

Ark Earth Online had never had a map function, even though it seemed like it should have been essential for a game set in such a vast world. The only maps that initially existed were rough continental drawings sold at prices far beyond the reach of beginner players in the Initial Three Kingdoms—the ones who would need them most. As the game evolved, players figured out how to create more detailed maps. Even those were a pain to use because they still had to be taken out and unfolded to be viewed, just like a real medieval map. They didn't mark your current location with a cursor, either.

"Right. If you have a map, you should probably take a moment to move it to the *Special Items* box," said Solomon.

Immediately, Mira went digging into her Item Box, but unfortunately, she didn't have any maps on her. "Ah, that's right. I left them all on my Floating Island."

"Welp. There's your problem."

Danblf had used the Floating Island as a sort of flying storeroom for trips to dungeons, helping to keep his Item Box free of clutter. It seemed to be the obvious place to keep maps—like keeping one in the glove box of a car.

But that raised another important question.

"By the way, I don't see the *Cash Shop Management* menu."

Solomon smiled grimly and bitter regret loomed in his voice. "That's because the Cash Shop is gone. Along with the *Inbox*, *Shutdown*, and *Log Out* options."

Cash Shop did exactly what it stated: it allowed players to access their purchases. It was how players traveled to and from their Floating Islands. There was no way for Mira to get her maps and other essential items.

"What...?!"

"I feel you. I had every type of holy sword on my Floating Island... It still hurts to think about it."

For a short while, the two of them gazed off into nothing, taking a moment of silence for their lost items. The Ethereal lamps cast their shadows across the wall with a flickering light.

"So. After figuring out who I was, you sent that urgent invitation for an audience?" Mira asked once the shock wore off a little.

"Yep. And the timing couldn't be more perfect. You look a little different, but that's what happens when you play around with a Vanity Case." Solomon returned to the issues of the moment, happy to forget about the loss of his Floating Island.

"I never would have used it if I knew this was going to happen..."

"If you liked the old man so much, why'd you change? You were always taking those cool screenshots and everything, making collections of your favorite poses."

"Well, I just...it's a long story."

Mira told him the story—from the email notice that her Cash Shop credits were about to expire, to how her curiosity drove her to check each and every one of the available parts for character creation. She skipped the part about this being her ideal female form.

"Woof. What a disaster." Solomon face showed just a hint of compassion for her plight.

"Indeed. I don't even remember accepting the change. I passed out midway through."

"You must have been really into it."

"I didn't even notice I pulled an all-nighter." Mira realized her mistake before she even finished speaking. She'd been friends with Solomon for long enough to know he could read between the lines. His smirk widened.

"You put a lot of effort into little Mira, there."

"...She is my greatest creation."

"Ha! I knew it! She's right up your alley." A grin twisted onto Solomon's mouth like a cat who just swallowed a canary.

The two of them had often spent nights discussing favorite idols or characters that they liked. He knew her tastes well, and saw straight through her attempt to play it off. And realizing that her current form was just a walking checklist of her proclivities, she slumped back over the sofa.

"Please tell me you have a spare Vanity Case," she implored.

"I do! See?" He produced the Japanese-style black lacquered box with a flourish. It was glorious. For a moment, Mira stared at the box, dumbstruck. Then she was on her feet, lunging at Solomon.

"Give it!"

"Whoa!" Solomon was knocked from his chair by her flying leap. Knickknacks and papers on his desk were scattered across the floor with an impressive clatter as she slid across it, grabbing for the Vanity Case.

"King Solomon, what is the matter?!" roared Reynard. He threw the door open, only to come to a standstill at the scene laid out before him.

The two were rolling on the floor, Mira straddling Solomon like a horse. She clutched his hand, which was also holding the Vanity Case. Any notion that this was an attack was dispelled by the placement of Solomon's other hand, planted firmly on her right breast. His leg had somehow gotten tangled in the hem of her robes, pushing it up to expose her lower half.

"No problem here, Reynard," Solomon said, trying to remain calm and keep a straight face.

"Aha! The witch has revealed her true colors!" Reynard leapt to the obvious conclusion, as usual.

"Come now, Sir Reynard." Joachim said, poking his head into the room a moment later to rein his partner back in. "Calm down and let's assess the situation? Please note the position of King Solomon's hand. He's giving her...quite the *massage*."

Reynard's eyebrow twitched in anguish. "Ugh, that's true... But..."

Joachim held up a hand to forestall the argument, then continued with his reasoning. "I have deduced that they were bonding while seated on the chair, and excessive motion caused them to lose their balance and topple. I admit that I had always assumed King Solomon had no interest in women—but it seems he may simply prefer those who match his own appearance. Understanding at last. Rejoice, Reynard! This will finally secure the future of our nation."

As Joachim admonished Reynard, his smile showed that he was enjoying this conversation immensely.

"Surely there must be someone better than this...girl!"

"She's the pupil of Master Danblf. Who could be more prestigious than that?"

"Hmm, that's true..." Reynard grudgingly admitted. As the two worked their way through the logical implications of the situation, Mira and Solomon finally realized what position they'd wound up in.

Mira's face was pressed close to Solomon's as she straddled him. Solomon had something soft and extremely pleasant to the touch in his hand. Simultaneously, the summoner and the king jumped as far away from each other as they could get.

"Hold it right there, you two! You've got the wrong idea!" Mira shouted.

"Yes, exactly! Mira fell over and I just got caught up in it. No impropriety has occurred!"

The two old friends hurriedly tried to straighten themselves, but the damage was done, and they had no chance of dissuading Reynard and Joachim from what they had just witnessed.

"As you say, sir. But King Solomon, I am going to have to ask you to behave responsibly," admonished Joachim unnecessarily.

"For the Kingdom... For an heir..." murmured Reynard, envisioning the future of Alcait as the two made their way from the office and closed the door behind them.

"I'll schedule an emergency meeting later," sighed Solomon.

"Looks like you've got some explaining to do."

"You're going to be there too. Don't think this doesn't concern you."

"It won't, once I use that Vanity Case," Mira pointed at the box Solomon was still holding, desperate to put an end to her predicament.

"Oh, ha. That's not going to work. This is a Cash Shop item."

"Of course it will work. I'm aware that it must be a priceless item now, so I will pledge my services and loyalty to you wholeheartedly if you let me use it. Hand it over." Mira reached toward the box like a kitten trying to snatch a piece of dangling yarn.

"Nope! First rule for Cash Shop items: They can't be transferred between players." Solomon held out the Vanity Case to Mira.

She tried to take it from Solomon's hand but her fingers slashed at the air in vain, passing through the box as if she were trying to grab a hologram.

"...What?! No!"

She
Professed
Herself
Pupil of the
Wise Man

12

"**B**UT...WHY?!" Mira stared in disbelief as her hand passed back and forth through the Vanity Box.

"I just told you. This world is real, but the original game rules are still in effect. Cash Store items are nontransferable, and it's still tied to my account. Things like Master Keys have owner's rights—we can *give* them to other people, but they can't be taken by force."

"You're saying there's nothing I can do unless I figure out how to get back into the Cash Shop?" Mira leaned in close and squinted suspiciously at the box.

"Yep. These items are hard to come by."

"Oh, hell..." Mira flopped face first onto the sofa. Her brain, overrun with emotion, frantically tried to come up with something that would work. She turned just her head, faintly clinging to a glimmer of hope. "Are there any work-arounds?"

"I've been here thirty years, and I haven't found any yet."

"Oh, *hell*..." The weight of the reply shattered any remaining hope. Mira lay on the sofa remembering her former glory, now gone forever.

"I wish I could give it to you, but I can't."

"Sure, sure. I bet you're going to giggle like a madman as soon as I leave the room." Mira was doing her best to emulate a sulky child as she pouted away with all her might.

"I'm being honest. You never gave up on our kingdom, did you? You and the rest of the Elders—it was your protection that put us on equal footing with the big players. How could I ever laugh at a hero like you?"

Solomon tried desperately to maintain a blank expression, but Mira didn't miss the tiny quiver at the corners of his mouth.

"Riiight..."

"Sorry. I'm sorry. But I really do wish I could give it to you," said Solomon, giving Mira a soft smile. Mira responded with a glare. Solomon averted his gaze and he attempted to change the subject. "Speaking of which, I'm assuming you've heard that the other Elders are missing?"

"Yes, Graia filled me in. He said that they all vanished around the same time. But he also told me that Luminaria returned twenty years ago. That's why I went to the towers first, to find out more about what happened."

"Good. Then I can skip that part of the story. But what do you think would become of our country without you guys?" Solomon asked in the tone of a quiz show host, but a shadow passed across his smiling face.

"I see the problem..." It was easy to imagine. Mira narrowed her eyes and stroked her chin.

The Kingdom of Alcait relied on the Nine Wise Men to

avoid war with neighboring countries. The country was rich, the king wasn't greedy, and by focusing on national defense, they had encouraged trade instead of provoking needless border conflicts.

When those pillars of support vanished, they left a country that was ripe for the picking. Luminaria was still around, but that was a heavy load for a single person to bear. And the rest of the world had known of the disappearances for at least twenty years. A series of skirmishes when their neighbors went after valuable resources were slowly exhausting the kingdom's military resources.

But if the Nine Wise Men were to return—or even just one of them—the country's reputation as a defensive force would come back. Especially if that one was Danblf, the One-Man Army renowned for his skills in mass combat.

"Now, this is just my opinion as king, but you are one of the heroes of this nation and your presence alone will have a tremendous influence. The problem is that we can't go shouting from the rooftops that you've turned yourself into a cute girl."

"Euugh..." There was nothing else Mira could say to that.

"You've still got the same abilities, but the optics are a problem. If you had always looked like this, it might not be an issue, but when people hear the name Danblf, they think of a grizzled veteran mage...someone who fits the image of a Wise Man."

Mira was flattered by the praise for Danblf's avatar and rose from the couch to strike a victory pose. She turned to Solomon with a joyful look.

"I'm sure they do. He was my masterpiece."

"And what do you think they'd make of their hero turning into...this?" Solomon gestured at her and smiled ruefully. Mira could only imagine.

"...I wouldn't believe a word of it," she muttered, completely cognizant of her own situation.

"Uh-huh. As much as I'd love to announce that Danblf has returned, I can't expose you for that reason alone. The people of this world don't know about Vanity Cases. They wouldn't understand."

"Hrmmm. Can we just announce it without me needing to make an appearance?" Feeling like she'd just struck on a brilliant idea, Mira suddenly popped up on the sofa.

"That'd be a tough sell. A legendary hero returns after thirty years—there'd be parties held throughout the country, and it's hard to throw a party without a guest of honor. Once things settled down, other countries would start sending reconnaissance parties to see for themselves."

Her brilliant idea slashed to pieces, Mira slumped back on the sofa and rolled over. Solomon was right. There would be celebrations, spies, and all sorts of other complications. If Danblf didn't appear, confidence in the Alcaitian government would plummet both at home and abroad.

But Solomon had no intention of announcing Danblf's return. There were more pressing matters at hand, and he had other plans for his old friend. Mira sat up and looked at him with a questioning gaze—his usual smile belied the serious look in his eyes.

But before he could speak, a commotion came from the corridor—the raised voice of Reynard. Solomon moved to the door to check the situation and found a military messenger bearing a note from the kingdom's national defense department.

"What's going on?" he asked in a low, calm voice full of regal dignity—a far cry from the tone he'd been using with Mira. Reynard and Joachim both bowed and stepped aside, and the messenger was briefly startled to see King Solomon at the door. He bowed and began to deliver his report.

"Sir, news from Fort Benedict. They've detected a horde of monsters moving to the northwest. They estimate there are around two hundred of them, made up of over thirty different species."

Report delivered, the messenger took a step back and stood at attention, awaiting further orders. His labored breath left no doubt that he'd rushed to deliver the news. Mira noticed that Reynard and Joachim showed visible unease, which she took as a bad sign.

"If they've made it to Fort Benedict, they're already in the country. How did the border guards miss a horde of that size?!" demanded Reynard.

"We just had one yesterday as well. This is far too soon. The diverse number of species is also a first. How curious." Joachim calmly analyzed the situation while wearing a grim expression.

"One day apart, a mixed group... Hmmm, excuse me for a moment." Solomon returned to his office. Solomon had evidently noticed something—Joachim hadn't missed the small smile on the king's face. As soon as the door shut, Solomon turned to Mira, where she'd been listening in from the sofa.

"Dan...er, Mira. I've got a job for you."

"But I'm still tired from the carriage ride." Mira whined. She could surmise what the request was going to be and she quickly began massaging her calves.

"Oh, suck it up! It can't be anyone but you! I beg of you."

"Fiiine. Leave it to me!"

It was like they were acting in a play and knew all the lines by heart. Solomon smiled widely. Ask, refuse, beg, agree—it was a sequence of dialog the two always performed whenever one asked the other for a favor, and it had been thirty years since Solomon last partook. He closed his eyes as he laughed, getting lost in the memories.

"It's been far too long since I've been able to do that. I really missed it."

"Maybe for you. For me, it was just last week. You asked me to go with you to the Shield Gate to gather materials."

"The Shield Gate! I *remember* that! If I recall correctly, we didn't get what we were after."

"We can walk down Memory Lane later. This is urgent, right? What do you need me to do?"

"Oh, right, um..." Solomon was brought back to the present by Mira's words. Wise Man Danblf had another ability, one that rivaled even his summoning techniques. "Do you happen to have any of your Magic Stones on you?"

"Of course. A complete collection." Mira replied as though the answer should have been obvious. "Never leave home without them."

A Magic Stone was a general term for any mineral that held power, but usually it meant magic-imbued gemstones. They could be found in nature, but Danblf had pioneered the technique of creating artificial Magic Stones through use of the Refining skill.

"Perfect! That's perfect. I'm so glad you showed up." The smile on his face was a blend of the joy of seeing an old friend and the relief of a king who knew he'd fulfil his responsibilities. To Mira, it was a familiar sight, and it reassured her that this was still the Solomon she remembered.

"Okay, I'll have the details explained to you en route, all right?"

"Hrmmm, okay."

Solomon grandly threw open the door. After taking a moment to snicker at the look of surprise on the faces of his three waiting subordinates, he began handing out orders. The messenger bowed before rushing off, followed by Reynard, who left to follow his instructions.

"I've arranged a special vehicle to take you to the site," said Solomon as he beckoned to Mira. Then he turned to Joachim. "Show her the way."

"At once, Your Majesty," replied Joachim with a graceful bow. He turned to Mira and bowed again.

"Well, I'm off."

"I'll leave it to you."

Joachim was amazed at the level of trust present in their tone. It didn't seem like they had only just met. He recalled a line he'd heard ever so faintly through the office door: *It can't be anyone but you!*

With his mind filled with a grand sense of misunderstanding, he led Mira to the garage where her ride was being readied.

The garage was in a basement level beneath the palace and used solely to house special carriages and other vehicles. As Mira was ushered into the cavernous room, she found herself standing before a black, matte-finished vehicle that looked incredibly modern and somehow familiar. It was covered in armored plating and had what appeared to be a gun barrel peeking out from a turret on the roof. She had little doubt that this armored car was the special vehicle that Solomon had mentioned.

"I see he's still into his toys."

"Isn't it marvelous?" Garrett's voice startled Mira. It seemed that he'd be her driver on this trip as well. "I didn't think I'd see you again so soon."

"The privilege is all mine." Mira's eyes narrowed as she shifted her gaze to Garrett. He blushed, opened the heavy-looking door of the armored car with a quick bow, and gestured her inside. "If you please, Miss Mira."

The interior of the vehicle was divided into front and rear compartments like a standard family car. A plush, extremely well-padded sofa had been installed in the back. Mira lightly rapped her knuckles on the car's armor as she entered, then sank deep into the soft couch. The rest of the interior was tastefully decorated with leather and wood paneling.

"Ho ho! This is quite a bit more comfortable than the exterior would suggest."

"We found it to be...necessary, actually," Garrett responded with a worried smile as he watched Mira bounce up and down on the sofa, checking its elasticity.

The armored car roared out of the palace garage and went blasting down the road leading to Fort Benedict.

Typical Solomon. If anyone in this world was going to build a wild machine like this, of course it's him, Mira thought as she observed the car in motion.

The speed of the car far surpassed that of the coach that brought her to the palace. Mira turned her attention from the scenery flying past the windows to look at Garrett up front; he was in the driver's seat, surrounded by a host of gauges and panels, cheerfully gripping the steering wheel beneath white knuckles.

"This thing looked pretty heavy, but it's actually quite quick, isn't it?" observed Mira as she looked out the windshield. It was a narrow horizontal slit that stretched from side to side, providing a wide panoramic view of the grassland and an occasional cluster of trees. Far out in the distance, she could make out a tall white pillar jutting unnaturally high into the sky.

"This is the product of our cutting-edge technomancy!" Garrett said excitedly. Despite the fact that he was facing forward, Mira could tell he was beaming.

"Technomancy?" Mira asked, and Garrett's enthusiasm turned up another notch as he began to explain.

"Indeed! Isn't it amazing? We use different combinations of metal parts to harness the power locked away within Magic Stones."

"Hmm... So, this uses Magic Stones, does it?"

"Correct. And this FAV, short for Fast Armored Vehicle, was just recently completed. It's the newest of the new!" The excitement in Garrett's voice continued to ramp up. "Unfortunately, it also consumes significantly more power from the Magic Stones than the earlier models, so we've only been able to give it one test drive."

"But they just handed me a whole pile of Magic Stones, telling me that I could use them as I pleased. The only order was to deliver you to your destination as quickly as possible. So it's all thanks to you, Miss Mira!" He quickly turned his head as he expressed his gratitude, then turned back to keep his eyes on the road.

So that's why Solomon was asking about Magic Stones.

While Garrett was somewhat surprised at the preferential treatment being granted to the Wise Man's pupil, he was nonetheless ecstatic to get a chance to push the FAV to its limits. After Danblf vanished, there'd been no one able to pick up the slack in Magic Stone manufacturing, and the once-plentiful Magic Stones became a precious commodity.

It seemed that the king was willing to splurge a little. If it got them to their destination as swiftly as possible, then all the better.

Garrett's passion for vehicles was unsurpassed, and that passion played a large role in his promotion to be the vice commander of the Mobile Armored Division. Now that he had been given the chance to test the limits of his favorite amongst favorites—the FAV—he was going to make it count. He fed another Magic Stone into the car's fuel box.

As they drove along, Garrett chattered away, listing detailed specifications and design features of the vehicle. The performance of the FAV was quite a bit better than Mira had imagined. It used the power of the Magic Stones to reinforce the strength of its frame, and could probably run over a few monsters without feeling a thing. Hardly any strain was placed on the body as it raced down the unpaved road, with no attention paid to the speed limit.

Hardly any strain was placed the on *vehicle*. The same could not be said for the *occupants*.

"Can't you...do something about this?!" Mira shouted as she bounced about the sofa. They had turned off of the paved road and were now speeding down a dirt trail through the middle of the grassland.

The FAV was a blend of all the latest technomancy developments, including a magic-powered radio device that connected to various ground stations across the country. The device allowed them to receive updates that confirmed the monsters were heading straight for something, instead of milling about aimlessly. What they were after was a mystery—there was no settlement in that direction, just grasslands and forest. But after a few more reports, they seemed to be approaching the towering white pillar and the field of flowers that surrounded it.

Mira frowned. That must be their target. The FAV was making a beeline for it across the uneven terrain, and it shook violently—sometimes even launching itself into the air. With each bounce, Mira went flying, only to be caught by the sofa. The seemingly opulent upholstery provided a necessary function.

"I can see the flower field ahead. We're almost there!" There was no stopping Garrett. The FAV plowed through open grassland.

"Hrmmm...so...we're...almost...there." Mira struggled to stay in her seat, trying to peek through the windshield at their destination. Monsters notwithstanding, she was looking forward to walking among the flowers after the ride ended.

The FAV crested a hill blanketed in fresh greenery and caught air going over the top. Garrett cheered, enjoying the momentary sensation of weightlessness.

The bottom of the slope opened into a dense meadow with scattered trees. Far in the distance lay a beautiful, circular field of flowers. In the center stood a pure white pillar, like a massive sword thrust into the earth.

"Looks like I was right." Mira had managed to get a grip on the arm of the sofa so she could stare out of the windshield.

The pillar was twice the height of the Linked Silver Towers, and there was movement on the edge of the forest surrounding the flower field. She was still too far away to make out the details of the horde, but based on their disorderly advance toward the tower, she could tell they were monsters.

"At this distance, it looks like they'll beat us there," she said. Even with the speed of the FAV, it seemed unlikely that they would arrive before they reached the structure. "Oh, well. Do what you can."

"As you wish!" replied Garrett as he thrust three Magic Stones into the fuel box in one go. The FAV whined and accelerated across the bumpy terrain.

Mira quickly amended her prior statement. "Do what you can—but *safely*!"

The FAV hurtled down the gentle slope, through the thick grass and into the trees. In just a few minutes, they'd closed the distance and were near enough that they could make out the individual monsters.

Mira focused on the monsters as an excuse to avoid looking at Garrett. His eyes gleamed with fanatic intensity as he held the wheel in a death grip. She noticed something.

"Wait, what are they doing?"

The monsters had been marching toward the field as a purposeful unit, even if they were a bit disorganized. Then they inexplicably stopped, readied their weapons, and fell upon one another in a pitched battle. Even those of the same species attacked their kin without regard to alliance or race. While it was true that sometimes monsters preyed on other monsters, they never attacked their own type, and they would never march together with their prey.

"What on earth...? Quickly, Garrett!" Mira cried. *Is there something out there that they're fighting over? Or perhaps...*

Whatever their intentions, something was afoot. As Mira rolled about on the sofa, she felt an inexplicable sense of dread.

The FAV came to a stop and Mira jumped out, slamming the heavy door open. She spotted the culprit. Among the monsters stood a singular crooked being, its body covered in scars.

"A Lesser Demon... Now this begins to make sense."

The monsters continued killing each other and their numbers dwindled. Finally, one remained victorious, and the Lesser Demon lopped off its head as a reward.

"Well, that's unsettling," muttered Mira.

The demon stood, cackling madly in the flower garden. Disgusted, Mira immediately summoned her Dark Knight.

The moment the spirit appeared, it charged across the landscape of fallen corpses to cut the fiend in two. A black mist billowed from the wound before diffusing into the air. Beneath the cloud, the carcass of the Lesser Demon fell to join the multitude of other bodies on the ground. Its face was still warped into a malicious grin.

"This isn't good," said Garrett, looking around as he caught up with Mira and her summoned spirit. The colorful flowers were now coated in the filth of the monsters' blood, like maidens whose purity had been defiled. Thankfully, most of the field remained unsullied. Only the outer perimeter had been ravaged, and the very center was still pristine.

"Well, time to head back and make a report," he sighed, regretting that he was unable to test the FAV's weapons system. "I suppose we should do something about these bodies first. If we leave them like this, we'll have to deal with ghouls later."

In the game world, the corpses of monsters would disappear after a few minutes had elapsed. Mira knew it was no longer that simple. She thought back to just after she'd arrived—the knights had burned the bodies of the goblins slaughtered by the Dark Knight.

"Indeed." Mira heaved a sigh at the thought of them having to drag all these bodies into a pile by themselves.

Glancing at the vast amount of corpses at their feet, Garrett announced he had just the thing before running back over to the FAV. A few moments later, he returned, two sachets in his hands.

"First, let's get them all into one pile. Miss Mira, if you could help me by sprinkling this over the bodies?" He offered her one of the sachets.

"Hrmmm, what's this?" The sachet contained a white powder. Doing as she was asked, Mira began spreading a handful over the corpses at her feet.

"Not too much! Just a pinch of Hamelin's Ashes will do." Garrett began to trot through the flower field, sprinkling the ashes over the dead monsters.

Mira followed his lead. His answer didn't actually explain anything, but she was sure she'd get the details later. A few minutes later, the job was complete. The two returned to stand beside the FAV.

"Right, let's finish this up and head home, shall we?" Garrett stepped into the center of the killing field and placed a square stone on the ground. As he jogged back, the strangest sight played out before Mira. The monsters, all still very much dead, began to rise to their feet and walk.

For a moment, Mira was on guard, nervously preparing to resummon the Dark Knight. But as she saw Garrett's calm demeanor, she relaxed and watched the dead-eyed creatures converge on the stone and fall over one another into a heap. Only a few minutes later, they'd formed a mountain of corpses.

"There we go, now we can burn them. Miss Mira, stand back just a bit, please."

"Let's see...what did I do with that Fire Attuned Magic Stone... Ah! There we go," Garrett leapt into the FAV's turret and pointed the muzzle at the pile of bodies. "And fire!"

There was a roar, and a beam of light shot from the gun toward its target. A moment later, the corpses erupted into a pillar of flame that reached high into the sky.

"That's incredible," mumbled Mira as she stared at the sparks flickering from the burning pyre. Turning to see the pure joy on Garrett's face, she laughed wryly to herself.

Though they had not arrived in time, the horde was neutralized. As the FAV rolled away from the flower field, Mira peeked back through the rear window. The ominous smile of the Lesser Demon lingered in her mind. What was its purpose?

She looked at the massive ivory tower, growing smaller in the distance.

CHAPTER 12

"Hrmmm? Wasn't it whiter before?"

The pillar stood undamaged, but to Mira's eye, it seemed a touch darker than when they'd arrived.

She
Professed
Herself
Pupil of the
Wise Man

13

Mira wedged herself back into the corner of Solomon's office sofa.

"How was the ride back?" he asked.

"Hrmmm. It was sort of like sitting on this couch, but with more opportunity for head trauma," she replied. She put her feet up on a pile of documents and opened another bottle of apple au lait. Garrett had driven with the same reckless abandon on the return trip, much to her chagrin.

"It's upsetting to hear that a Lesser Demon was behind this. You really think that it managed to achieve its objective?"

"No doubt about it. I heard the cackle before the Dark Knight cut it down." Mira put the half-full bottle on the table and shuddered as she recalled the Lesser Demon's final, eerie smile. Its cackle was something that any former player would recognize, a sure signal that the enemy had achieved victory.

Thirty years ago, events involving Lesser Demons never went well—most of them ended up as mitigated failures at best.

Solomon had firsthand experience with this, and he looked over the finalized report with an annoyed expression.

"Troubling, but I don't need another nuisance added to my plate right now. I'm just too busy."

"So I'm a nuisance now, eh?" Mira needled the king.

"No, no, of course not. Actually, you being here solves some of my problems. Going back to what we were discussing before, the thing about not being able to announce you as a Wise Man right away..."

"Yeah, I remember that."

"I have a suggestion." Solomon put the report he'd compiled on the desk, laced his fingers together, and leaned forward—like a certain familiar administrator. It was a common pose for when they needed to have a serious conversation.

"Oh, it's that big of a deal, eh? Looks like I've touched a NERV. Get it?" Mira said with a dumb grin that faded quickly. "Eh, never mind. Shoot."

"I think that we can get away with declaring you as Danblf's pupil and successor to the title of Elder. And as long as you do something outstanding, people will have to agree."

It made sense. If they could pad her resume a little, then it would give her the social capital to take up her former duties and influence the direction of the nation. Once she had a solid track record, it shouldn't cause any hard feelings among the rest of the mages that might have had their eye on the position.

"It would totally work," Solomon said with a slight smile that faded a little as he pondered just how difficult the task would be. "Probably. It's worth a try, anyway. Would you please consider it?"

"Well, okay. How do you think I should do this?"

Solomon took a deep breath and crossed his arms. Unlike his usual mischievous self, there was a small trace of worry on his face.

"Danb—no. I'm going to have to start calling you Mira. I can't afford any slipups."

"That's fair."

"All right, Mira. I have a task that I can't ask of anyone else. I need you to find everyone."

"...Everyone?" Mira repeated the word slowly while her hand stroked her chin. The word floated for a moment, and then it all made perfect sense. Her brow wrinkled and she shot Solomon a troubled look.

"Luminaria and myself aren't the only ones online, are we?"

"Bingo. In fact, you were the last to return."

"What...?"

"I showed you how to access your Friends List. See for yourself."

Mira toyed with her bracelet. Pulling up the secondary screen, she opened her Friends List where all of her comrades' names were gathered. Solomon and Luminaria's names were displayed in white, as were the other names she was looking for. The seven other Elders who, alongside herself and Luminaria, made up the Nine Wise Men...were all listed as online. She scanned the list and tried to tamp down the rising nostalgia.

"Hrmmm... Looks like the gang's all here."

"So it seems."

"Okay, where are they?" Mira realized she'd been found through some fast detective work on Solomon's part, but this was a serious mystery.

"I don't know, and that's why I want you to find them."

"That's going to be tough. I don't even know where to start. Aside from their towers, they were never the sort to stay in a fixed location."

"I'm sure it will take a while. But I'm hoping you'll find at least half of them before the year is out."

Half of them within the year—that sounded specific and ominous. Mira had known Solomon long enough that she could tell when he was holding something back. She decided it was time to manage some expectations.

"Before the end of the year? That's a tight deadline. I'm starting from nothing; not a single clue to go on. Maybe it's doable within a year or two."

"That may be, but it has to be done this year. You returned right in the nick of time. It must be fate." Solomon knew full well that what he asked wasn't a simple task.

He had no choice but to entrust the duty to his most capable friend and ally. The sight of such a young-looking boy with his eyebrows furrowed in such complete exhaustion was strange. Mira could tell that he was in dire straits.

"What's got you in such a hurry, Solomon? Spill it."

Solomon took a file from the collection on his bookshelves and spread it out over the table in front of the sofa. Skimming the title, she saw it was a record of a battle that had occurred ten years prior. The conversation Mira had with Graia floated back up in her mind.

"The…Defense of the Three Great Kingdoms?" After glancing at the contents, Mira checked the cover and muttered the title.

"Have you heard of it?"

"Yeah. Captain Graia mentioned it. Happened ten years ago. Monster attacks started increasing afterward."

"Yep. Without the Wise Men, the knights have been holding down national defense. And now the incursions are happening so often that my military budget is through the roof." Solomon sat down next to Mira and took a drink from the apple au lait on the table.

"It's been forever since I've had one of these."

"Hey! I don't want any of your royal backwash!"

"My blood ain't blue—they made me king, I wasn't born one. I'll never lose my love of junk food." He waved the empty bottle at her, signaling that he wanted a refill. Mira knocked aside the empty but still gave Solomon another bottle of apple au lait.

"So that's your reason to get me on this mission? Same old story. Get the Wise Men to do the dirty work and you get to cut your war budget."

"Well, yeah. That would be a massive help, but there's actually a more urgent issue." Solomon took a drink and flipped through the file, stopping at a certain page. It was titled *Limited Non-Aggression Pact*.

Mira figured it would be easier to ask for a summary than it would be to comb through the fine print. "Hrmmm, so what's this all about?"

"You weren't here, but the Defense of the Three Great Kingdoms was a war on a scale unmatched by anything we've ever experienced. Maybe it'd be easier for you to understand if I told you that the God-Kings of the Initial Three Kingdoms took to the field."

"You're kidding me... the Immovable Lords?!" Mira's surprise wasn't for nothing. The Initial Three Kingdoms were the beginner countries and had enjoyed a protected status ever since the game launched. They existed to ensure the safety of fledging players.

Even when the land rush was in full swing across the continent, no kingdom dared declare war on the Initial Three. These three nations were home to scores of overpowered NPC characters that could easily defeat even the highest-level players. Victory against them was impossible, and in turn, they never took sides in battles between player-run kingdoms. That was the tacit deal—player-run kingdoms left the Initial Three alone, and in turn, the Immovable Lords stayed immobile and didn't swat them like mosquitos.

If the kings of these three nations saw fit to go to war, Mira could only imagine the magnitude of the resulting battle.

"It was called the Defense of the Three Great Kingdoms because that's where the front line was drawn, but the war was waged across the entire continent. It began when a horde of demons descended from the sky. They started by attacking the Initial Three, but as they gained reinforcements, the front extended to other locations. Many smaller nations were destroyed outright. It was terrible."

Solomon's face twisted in anguish as he reflected. Mira hadn't been there, so she couldn't truly understand—but it was hard to watch her close friend remember a terrible past.

"Anyways, the point is there was a massive war ten years ago that nearly destroyed everything. The aftermath was about what you'd expect."

"Everyone must have been busy with reconstruction efforts."

"Exactly. And that's why we came up with the *Limited Non-Aggression Pact*. Simply put, it prohibited war and related aggressive activity for ten years after ratification. Everyone gets to focus on domestic spending rather than defense spending."

"And now you're telling me that time's almost up, right?" Mira made the logical jump. War might soon be an issue again.

If the Kingdom of Alcait had only one of their Nine Wise Men, that was an opportunity that other nations could take advantage of. With its bountiful lands and unrivaled magical knowledge, the Kingdom of Alcait was a prize waiting to be seized.

"Honestly, the treaty is one of the only things protecting us at the moment. We need a fighting force that can defend our nation from attacks...and preferably deter them from happening in the first place. Mira, I need you to find the others for me."

Mira closed the file and took a breath. Deep down, she already knew her answer.

"Why not? I accept."

Solomon smiled broadly and clapped her on the shoulder. "Now that that's out of the way, we can tackle the issue of how and where to find them."

Draining the rest of his apple au lait, Solomon fidgeted with the bottle in his hands.

"That is the catch, isn't it? They're not the type to be easily found." Mira sighed, daunted by the task.

"Yep. But the thing about the Wise Men was that you were all slaves to your ideals. You were a bunch of oddballs with specific quirks and kinks." Solomon held up the empty bottle and placed his eye to the opening, peering at Mira like one might peer through a microscope. He had a wry grin. "Just look what happened to you."

Before Mira could respond, commotion filled the hallway outside. They could make out Reynard's voice pleading with someone to stop just before a woman burst through the door, barely leaving the hinges intact.

Entrance aside, everything about her demanded attention—her blue-and-white robes hugged her voluptuous figure, and her striking beauty would make anyone take notice. She ran her fingers through her fiery red hair, clearly unconcerned with how it sent her ample breasts swaying. Glancing at Solomon for a moment, she turned her bright red eyes to the other girl in the room.

"It's still too early for our set meeting." Solomon stared at the woman—his tone more dignified since the door was open.

In response, the woman slammed the door behind her, smacking Reynard in the face. He staggered back in agony with a bloody nose and tears in his eyes.

Joachim put a comforting hand on his friend's shoulder, saying, "There was nothing you could have done to stop her."

A cheerful smile decorated the woman's face she turned to Solomon. "I heard that some girl claiming to be Danblf's pupil arrived at the palace. I went to the guest rooms to meet her, but she wasn't there. So I tracked down a nearby guard and squeezed him for answers. He told me she was here, so here I am."

"I see. I had planned on introducing the two of you later, but I guess we're all here now," said Solomon as he walked over to stand beside Mira. "This is the girl in question, Danblf's...*pupil*. Her name is Mira."

After being introduced, Mira just stared at the woman instead of standing or offering a greeting of her own. Then she grinned at Luminaria's unchanged appearance and flopped back onto the couch.

"I see. King Solomon, do you think it wise to speak in such a casual manner?" The woman cast a suspicious glance at Mira.

"Oh, don't get your panties in a bunch. And you can drop the act—it sounds weird when you do it. Besides, she's actually Danblf," said Solomon as a mischievous smile stretched across his face.

"Wh...wh-what?!"

"Hey, Lumi, long time no see. Well, long time for you. It was like yesterday for me." Mira raised a hand from her relaxed position on the sofa.

"So you've finally decided to join us..." Luminaria moved around so she could get a look at Mira from all angles. Luminaria and Danblf had once discussed their preferences in women, and Mira's current appearance perfectly matched the content of that conversation. Both overjoyed to see her friend again and tickled pink at Mira's current state, Luminaria burst into laughter.

The faint sound of laughter carried through the closed door and out in the hallway. Reynard covered his ears, sharing a nod with Joachim. There was a rumor floating about the palace that sometimes Luminaria seemed like an entirely different person. She was spooky.

After her fit of laughter subsided, Luminaria stared at Mira and smirked evilly.

"So you've finally come over to other side, eh? Taken the new ride for a test drive yet?"

She opens her mouth and goes straight to vulgarity, thought Mira. But in all fairness, that was a part of Luminaria's charm. It wouldn't do to let her know that, though. "I'm not some degenerate like you, Lumi. This was an accident. It was not my decision."

"Looks like a lot of work went into that accident and you're awfully defensive about it..." Luminaria ran her hand through Mira's silver hair and then hooked a finger on her collar, pulling it back so that she could take a peek inside to confirm that everything was indeed perfect.

"Ugh. It's a long story." Mira shoved Luminaria's hand away in exasperation and then explained everything that had happened, all the way from the email to the present.

"I bought my Vanity Case for the same reason. But I didn't use it," said Solomon. Mira wasn't sure if that was damnation or a defense.

"Yeah, me too." Luminaria pulled her own Vanity Case out of her Item Box and let it rest on her palm.

Mira glared at them with unbridled envy before plopping back down on the sofa to pout. "Why am I the only one who doesn't have one?"

"Because you used it." Solomon's blunt words skewered her argument, and with a groan, she lay back on the sofa. She kicked out her arms and legs, looking for all the world like a petulant child.

"But hey, all's well that ends well, right?" Luminaria said, trying to cheer her up. "At least you didn't make some joke character. You made an avatar that you actually like, right? It's like a blessing in disguise. Let me tell you, when this world became real, I was stoked. I spent my entire first day just getting to...*grips* with my new body."

An alluring smile with a hint of lewdness graced her beautiful face. It would have charmed any man so long as they didn't know what it concealed. Unfortunately, the other two people in the room were well aware of her proclivities.

Mira turned an icy stare on Luminaria, who hadn't changed a bit, and a question popped into her mind. "So I just thought of something. Solomon's been here for thirty years, and you for twenty, right? Then why don't either of you look any different? You haven't aged at all."

Mira had the excuse of only being in the new world for a couple of days, but it puzzled her that the other two seemed exactly the same as when she'd last seen them. She could give Luminaria a pass, but definitely not Solomon. How could someone nearing their forties still look like a young boy?

"Oh, right. I forgot about that." Solomon rolled his office chair over toward the sofa so that he could sit while he talked. Luminaria swiftly claimed it, crossing her long slender legs in a calculated attempt to show them off.

"That's just one of the things that makes this world so amazing," she said with a grin.

"I'll keep it simple," Solomon spoke as he repeatedly poked the back of Luminaria's head in retaliation. "In this world we—the former players, that is—are different from the regular folk who used to be NPCs."

"How so?"

"Well, for starters, Inspecting. Have you tried to Inspect me or Luminaria yet?"

Mira thought back to the audience in the throne room. No information had been displayed when she'd Inspected Solomon. Deciding to give it another try, she focused on Luminaria, who was squirming around in the chair as she tried to avoid Solomon's pokes. Just the same, no information appeared.

"Nothing shows up for either of you. It worked on Suleiman and Graia, though."

Solomon laughed and settled himself down on the couch near Mira's sprawled-out legs.

"It seems the Inspect action doesn't work on former players," he said. "That's just one of the differences. By the by, I tried Inspect on you when we met and didn't see anything either. That was another way I could tell you were a former player. That, plus your status switching to online, and a girl perfectly fitting your... *tastes* showing up claiming to be Danblf's pupil? That was enough circumstantial evidence to convict."

"So you're saying it can be used as a method of detection—it can tell me what kind of person I'm looking at, even if it won't tell me *who* I'm looking at," Mira said with a bitter smile.

"Yep. We don't know if the people we're looking for have changed appearance or not. This will at least tell us whether they're players." As he spoke, Solomon tugged down Mira's robe, which had ridden up to expose her drawers.

Mira swatted his hand away. "And knowing their personalities, we should be able to judge them based on more than just appearance."

"Probably. I could probably recognize Luminaria no matter what she looked like."

"Indeed. There aren't many S-Class perverts like her."

They both looked over at Luminaria, who was absorbed in ogling her own legs. She'd glared at them for a moment before shrugging to acknowledge that she couldn't deny it.

"If you can recognize me even when I don't look like me, that means we must be the bestest friends ever!" Luminaria said before leaping to her feet and diving onto the sofa like a professional wrestler. Solomon managed to roll out of the way, leaving an exhausted Mira to bear the brunt of Luminaria's affection. "Buddies forever and ever and ever!"

"Whoa! Knock it off, Loony-naria! What do you think you're touching?!"

Luminaria's grasping hands wriggled about, trying to find every nook and cranny to tickle and poke. "Come on, I'm just stoked to see you agai—ack!"

Luminaria had been winning the tickle fight when there was a dull thud. With a gasp that seemed to come from the pit of her stomach, she flew into the air, bounced off the ceiling, and crashed onto the floor. Still lying face-up on the sofa, Mira's right hand slowly returned to her side—she'd hit Luminaria with an immortal Sage technique at point-blank range.

"Looks like sexual harassment can be pretty risky, eh?" Solomon said, but as Luminaria staggered back to her feet, she gave a thumbs-up.

"Worth it."

"Do that again and I'll include a curse for your troubles." Mira got up, straightened her robes, and glared daggers at Luminaria.

Luminaria's hands, still hoping for action but finding nothing, started picking up the scattered papers on the floor.

"How thoughtful," said Solomon.

"Oh, you know me," said the buxom sorceress. "I just... I like things neat and tidy."

"Well, in that case, I'll leave you to your work." Solomon pointed at documents scattered over his desk and Luminaria nodded silently.

**She
Professed
Herself
Pupil of the
Wise Man**

"OKAY, BACK TO where we left off. The biggest difference between us and the former NPCs is our bodies. As you've noticed, we don't seem to age," said Solomon, spreading his arms and gesturing to himself.

"So that's why you haven't changed in thirty years."

"Yep. But the state of diagnostic medicine here isn't exactly modern, so I can't say that as absolute fact. Maybe we aren't aging. Or maybe we're aging internally, but not externally. Will we get geriatric diseases? What's our lifespan? All sorts of questions. We might not know for another forty to fifty years."

No wonder Luminaria thought this world was amazing—she was eternally beautiful here. Solomon's explanation made a weird sort of sense. It was some fundamental rule of this world that holdovers from the game were sacrosanct. Avatars never aged, so neither would we.

Thirty years was too soon for a natural death to come calling, but could they still die from other causes? When the world had been a game, death meant a free trip back to their home country and resurrection in a weakened state. Did the same rule apply now that the world was reality? She didn't want to know, but she *had* to know.

"So...what happens if you die in this world? Do you get resurrected?"

"Hmm, death..." Solomon folded his arms, a troubled expression on his face. After a few moments gathering his thoughts, he looked back up. "I honestly don't know for sure. I haven't heard of a player dying yet. This is just my personal opinion, but think that's the end of the road. Once you die, you're probably dead for good."

That seemed like a prudent and reasonable assumption, but she was curious as to his rationale. "What makes you think that?"

"It comes back to the Friends List. I check it every evening, and sometimes people just appear in this world, like you did. But there have been a few cases where the opposite has happened. I had a friend online but I had no idea where he was..." Solomon paused to wet his lips. The sound of Luminaria shuffling papers echoed through the room during the moment of silence. Then he continued. "One night, I was checking my Friends List and his status had changed to offline. And to this day, he hasn't been back online."

"I see..." said Mira. If being online on the Friends List meant you were present and being offline meant you weren't, there were two ways to interpret that. The first was that somehow they'd found a way to log off. But the second was that they'd vanished from the world the old-fashioned way—they were dead. Mira decided that it would be best to act with an abundance of caution going forward.

"Don't be so morose!" Luminaria piped up from where she sat on the desk, organizing papers. "When it comes to life or death for players, the most common cause is battle, right? We're not going to go out like that. On the off chance we come across something we can't beat, we just run away as fast as we can. Doesn't matter if it's a Beast Lord, a Demon Lord, or a Dragon Lord—we just keep right on living."

She was right—there wasn't much that posed a real threat to the three of them. They had been some of the strongest players in the game, and that meant they were some of the strongest beings in this world, period.

"And besides, this is all just speculation," she continued. "Let's put it aside for now. We don't need to find the answer. We just have to take care and watch each other's backs."

A smile returned to Solomon's face and he pulled up the menu from his bracelet to check the time.

"What do you guys say about taking a break so we can get some dinner? It's around that time." Solomon stood as he spoke and then cracked the door to convey his wishes to the two men waiting outside the office.

A short time later, a maidservant arrived to inform them that the meal was ready, and the three moved from the office to a large banquet hall. They were the hall's only occupants, so they continued to speak freely.

"Look at this spread! You're really leaning into being a king!"

Mira made the rounds with plate in hand, determined to sample every offering.

"Top-notch ingredients prepared by top-notch chefs. Only the best," bragged Solomon as he snagged a plate and lined up alongside Mira.

"Try the fried chicken. It is simply ah-mazing," said Luminaria as she placed a piece on Mira's plate before stuffing another directly into her mouth.

For Solomon and Luminaria, *top-notch* had become the standard. Mira's eyes lit up before the sumptuous feast, and her enthusiasm was infectious. Dinner at the palace was a joyful affair that evening.

After the meal, the three sat on the edge of the stage in the banquet hall and reminisced about the past.

"That was forever ago. I can still remember how cool they looked." Solomon's eyes were closed as he cast his mind back to an offline event he attended some thirty years ago. The Japanese Self-Defense Forces organized an annual exposition where attendees could view actual military equipment and weapons. It was initially held to boost recruitment numbers, but it ended up being an incredibly popular convention for military nerds. Solomon made sure to plan his schedule so that he could attend every year.

"The Type 10 battle tank. I wish I could go see it again." He kept his eyes closed, trying to visualize the vehicle.

"I could have done without all the walking. I swear, I walked more that day than any other day in my life," remembered Mira.

"Yeah, that sucked. I only tagged along because Solomon here said he'd cover the costs, but it was nothing but an army geek extravaganza."

While Luminaria playfully griped about the past, Mira smirked at Solomon's happy face as he lost himself in the memories.

"Oof, that's harsh." Solomon moped theatrically, his feet dangling in the air. "Come on, you know you two had fun."

From Mira's perspective, the event had only been about two weeks ago. Solomon had offered to treat them to a vacation, and they wound up in a giant event hall filled with rows of aircraft and weapons instead. With the memory of the event fresh in her mind, she suddenly thought of the FAV.

"By the way, what's with the armored car? It was running on Magic Stones instead of fuel and even had a flame-spewing cannon. Garrett said something about 'technomancy'?"

Mira's question brought the smile back to Solomon's face. and he stood up and moved to the center of the stage.

"I'm so happy you asked! The FAV is only the first step in my dream..." Solomon began to joyfully ramble on, declaring that as king, he would soon have his very own force of Type 10 battle tanks. The other two politely applauded when appropriate.

"...and thank you all for attending my lecture!" he finished with a flourish. As Solomon posed, arms outstretched, he glanced at the clock, which stood standing near the entrance to the banquet hall, and then jumped from the stage. "Oh! Perfect timing. It's time for our *meeting*."

"Oh, right. That's why I'm here, isn't it?" Luminaria said, as if only just remembering.

"What? Time for what meeting?" Mira asked as she was pulled sharply back to the present. The other two turned back to look at her with wide, confident smiles. Luminaria grasped Mira's hand and pulled her along.

"Just wait and see!" Solomon said in a playful tone. "This is going to change the world!"

The three made their way down countless flights of stairs. The silence grew with each passing floor, leaving nothing but the sound of their footsteps to reverberate off the cold, gray walls. Mira figured they must have gone down at least ten stories before they arrived at a large steel door flanked by guards.

Solomon and Luminaria received a standard military salute and a report that everything was in order.

"Understood, and well done," replied Solomon, back in king mode. Luminaria had also put her public interaction mask back on.

"Everyone has gathered, sir."

"Excellent."

"We're almost ready to begin. And who is your guest, King Solomon?" The guards turned to look at Mira.

"This is Danblf's pupil, Mira. She's joining us this evening, as her skills may prove useful in today's experiment."

"Of course, Your Majesty," the guard said, and then held a key card to the door. Slowly, the steel door opened, revealing a white corridor that continued onward.

Mira followed Solomon and Luminaria through the door. The medieval architecture of the palace was replaced by modern, state-of-the-art construction. As she glanced around, she was reminded of an aerospace facility she'd once seen on TV before.

These two have been up to something fun, it seems. Mira looked around and took stock. Underground base, heavy doors, experiments. Solomon had been hiding a secret research laboratory.

"Well, here we are." Solomon stopped before a large door that slowly began to open under its own power.

"Will you look at that," gawked Mira. Behind the door was a cavernous space painted dazzling white, so voluminous that the far end of the hangar was almost out of sight.

It was filled with countless machines and instruments, but one large object immediately caught Mira's eye. It had a thick, heavy base with a long tube jutting horizontally out of one side. Researchers in white coats monitored the various meters and gauges that surrounded it. Other technicians dressed in grease-stained coveralls stood near the unit and discussed something among themselves.

Standing near the door where Mira had entered was a group of eight mages and five nobles. Their lavish, baroque robes seemed out of place, given the surroundings.

"Thank you for your patience, King Solomon," said Suleiman. Solomon's attendant stepped out from beside the door and gave Mira a small bow before proceeding to his position at Solomon's side.

"Well done, everyone," Solomon's voice rang out. Workers nearby stopped and bowed as one to their king. As they lifted their heads, their gazes focused on the unfamiliar girl standing at his side.

Still unaccustomed to being the subject of curiosity, Mira shifted from foot to foot. But just as she was about to duck out of sight behind Luminaria, the sorceress grabbed Mira's shoulders and shoved her to the forefront.

"Let me introduce you all to Mira, Danblf's pupil. She has studied and mastered his refining techniques—I'm sure she will be useful for this experiment."

The revelation caused quite a stir, and one of the nobles stepped forward.

"This girl is Danblf's protégé?! I must introduce myself, with your permission, of course," came a voice from the group.

"Very well." With Solomon's blessing, the nobleman approached Mira and knelt before her.

He seemed to be somewhere between sixty and seventy years old with silver-gray hair and a heavily lined face that wore a gentle smile. He was the very embodiment of aged serenity and possessed a regal air that rivaled even Solomon's. His clothes were tasteful but not overly ostentatious.

"It is a pleasure to make your acquaintance. I am Edward

Corse Steiner. It is a great honor to meet the student of the great hero Danblf."

He concluded his greeting by taking her hand and gently kissing the back of it. Mira normally would have been compelled to brush that sort of thing away, but she found herself in awe of his dignified and gentlemanly demeanor.

"Uh...I'm Mira."

Edward stood, bowed, and returned to the other dignitaries. As Mira watched him walk away, she made a mental note to learn more about the man. She couldn't help but feel that she remembered his name from somewhere. But though she racked her brain, the memory sat like a reflection on a puddle of water, never quite taking shape.

No one present was quite sure why Luminaria was chuckling to herself.

"So are we prepared? Let's start with the first step." Solomon's voice returned Mira's focus to the present. She looked at the giant machine at the center of everyone's attention as engineers and researchers busied themselves with preparations.

"Looks like a bigger version of the weapon on top of the FAV," muttered Mira as she considered the long black tube that resembled a gun barrel.

"That was the prototype. This is the real thing," whispered Luminaria, taking the opportunity to get a better look at Mira's new body while most of the audience was focusing on something else.

A few researchers saw the smile that Luminaria gave Mira, and took it for a sign of sisterly affection—but alas, Mira knew what that smile hid. With a carefully blank face, she shifted a step or two further away from the ravishing sorceress. Out of the corner of her eye, she saw technicians setting up some sort of device downrange.

Mira craned her neck to get a better look, which set her silver hair fluttering and made her countless ribbons sway. The two men making final adjustments to the cannon's target noticed her noticing them.

"Hey, why's she staring at us?" noticed the researcher.

"What does it matter? Let's just hurry up and finish this."

"Yeah, but. I mean..."

"What's got you all worked up?" asked the engineer as he fine-tuned a valve.

"Well, she's Master Danblf's pupil..."

"Oh, you mean little Mira over there."

"Whoa, you can't just call her little. That's rude!"

"Well, she *is* little. What else should I call her?"

"I don't know. Maybe 'Miss Mira'?"

"Sure, fine. Hand me the 10mm socket."

The researcher smirked as the engineer shook his head in exasperation. Despite being focused on an absurd conversation, their pace increased, as her attention had them in high spirits. After a few more moments of calibration, the engineer stood and waved a flag to signal that their work was complete, and both men hustled to safety before the test began.

"Preparations complete. Ready when you are, sir," announced the chief engineer. Wearing a red hat so that he could be spotted by any of his crew, he stepped to a control panel and awaited the king's command.

Mira could tell that this was no ordinary cannon. Back in the game, players with blacksmithing skills had developed cannons. They fired iron shells using crude gunpowder and had been fairly common weapons in many countries. But they weren't nearly as big as this beast, and they didn't require the countless technical-looking instruments attached to it.

The little one on the FAV packed a punch. Let's see what this giant can do. Mira stroked her chin and waited for things to kick off.

Finally, everyone was in position.

"Start the experiment," commanded King Solomon.

"Start the experiment!" repeated the chief, throwing the switch that would divert power to the weapon.

The nobles gasped as the room was filled with the high-pitched whine of a motor and the instruments' needles began to tremble. Staring warily at the cannon, Reynard and Joachim moved to stand in front of Mira, Solomon, and Luminaria.

"First stage in five...four...three..." counted the chief as the whine grew higher pitched, joined by the occasional sound of electric discharge. "Two...one... Critical point confirmed!"

"Fire!" At Solomon's command, the engineer pushed a lever. A bolt of lightning shot from the muzzle, accompanied by a terrible roar. As the torrent of destruction smashed into a barrier of light expanding from the machine downrange, vibrations shook the room, and then after a moment, the sound of an explosion ripped through it. The target device had been wholly blown away, overwhelmed by the cannon's power.

The spectators in the room were stunned. The power of this new cannon far outstripped anything that Mira had seen before. Her eyes sparkled as she looked upon it.

"It's...it's glorious!"

Luminaria stood behind Mira, bracing her hands on the young woman's shoulders. She knelt down, bringing them cheek to cheek, and whispered, "We've been busy while you've been gone. Glad to see you like the Accord Cannon."

They stared at the destruction, admiring the progress.

15

THE TEST FIRING was a complete success, and the researchers began the slow process of analyzing the data. Meanwhile, key members of the team relocated to a nearby conference room to go through their documents and discuss future mass production efforts.

Mira managed to give these boring trivialities the slip and began to rummage through the various odds and ends on the shelves throughout the hangar.

"All right, Toma," Solomon said to the chief engineer. "It seems like the first stage activation was a success. There weren't any hidden problems?"

"None, Your Majesty. The recoil was completely suppressed. We might be able to raise the minimum output levels in future tests," responded Chief Toma confidently. Solomon nodded in satisfaction.

"The test was most impressive, Chief Toma. You can rest assured you have the full manufacturing support of the Wellesley family." One of the nobles leaned forward, and the others murmured their assent as well.

"On that subject..." Toma's expression clouded as he presented a document on the table before them. On it was written the steps needed to procure the necessary materials to power the cannon and produce its ammunition.

"As you can see here, each shot requires one Refining Stone as a projectile and two lightning-attuned Magic Stones as propellent," Toma explained. "With your support, mass production of the cannon assembly won't be a problem. The issue will be securing a reliable supply of Refining Stones and Magic Stones."

The Accord Cannon extracted the power sealed within the Magic Stones and amplified it before focusing the power into the Refining Stone until it reached critical power level. Then the Refining Stone exploded, directing the wild torrent of energy down the barrel. If refined materials of higher quality were used, more power could be channeled into the shot before they reached their critical point. This could affect the power and range of the cannon greatly.

Only a few people in the kingdom had the ability to create Refining Stones, and the materials that they produced were of middling quality at best. Ever the perfectionist, Toma was irritated that years of weapons development were being slowed by a supply chain issue. But even with mediocre ammo, the performance of the Accord Cannon was still unbelievable.

"I believe I have a solution." Solomon cheerfully placed a few faintly glowing gemstones on the table.

"Turquoise and moonstone? Well, these are Magic Stones...

But King Solomon, they're unrefined. How does this solve our problem?"

It was true, the gems that Solomon had produced were not particularly rare in any way, even if they did naturally store a small amount of magic power. Toma was puzzled, but had seen King Solomon pull this sort of trick before. He waited in curiosity for the king to continue.

"Miss Mira! If you'd be so kind?"

"What? What do you want?!" cried the girl in the corner of the room confusedly, drawing everyone's attention.

Solomon couldn't help but snort as he turned to see Mira being carried over, cradled to Luminaria's ample bosom and flailing as she tried to escape. Luminaria plopped her before the table, where Mira glared at the sorceress in indignation. Then Mira realized she was the center of attention and shrunk back.

"Well, what do you want?" Mira demanded, trying to gloss over what just happened and turning her glare to Solomon.

"Terribly sorry to disturb you. We were just hoping you could help." It was obvious from his smile that he was not sorry at all. Solomon reached out and picked up some of the gems from the table. "Mira, could you turn these into Refining Stones for us, please?"

The room's attention was locked onto his hand.

"Hmph, so that's why I got dragged along to this demonstration?"

Mira began to reach out for the gemstones, but her hands were filled with two misshapen figurines that she'd taken from a shelf. Her right hand held a red robot; her left hand, a blue robot.

Their inventory tag had indicated they could be combined to make a larger figurine, and she'd been puzzling over that process when Luminaria swept her up.

"Perhaps I could hold on to those for you, miss?" Suleiman swept in to fill the sudden awkward silence, and as he reached out from the side, Mira gently handed over the misshapen robot figures with a small clattering noise.

"Ugh. And I was just about to figure out how they worked," Mira grumbled under her breath before handing the toys over to Solomon's aide. "Thank you, Suleiman."

Mira accepted the gemstones just as Luminaria returned. She carried a folding table with odd designs carved into its top.

"Is that a refining station?" Toma asked. Though he wasn't a mage, he recognized the runes for dismantling, combining, transmuting, converting, and compressing etched into the wood.

"Are you going to start refining them right now? Won't that take some time?" Edward asked.

It was a fair question. Even the most skilled refiner in the kingdom took at least thirty minutes to create a single Refining Stone. The other nobles and mages who were familiar with the process nodded along at his question.

"Let's find out! Mira?" Solomon gestured to the mobile workspace.

Mumbling and grumbling to herself, Mira sat before the refining station. From the corner of her eye, she could see the robots in Suleiman's hands.

Oh, well. The faster I get this over with, the faster I can get back to it.

She placed the gemstones on the symbol of dismantling and then moved her hands into position. A moment later, they began to faintly glow.

Each gemstone had its own properties, but by mixing multiple gems together, it was possible to create a Refining Stone. Through subtle manipulation of power, she was able to dismantle the gemstones into their base components. Then she extracted only the materials that held power before compressing and recombining them. Amid shimmering, flickering light, the gemstones began to change and take on a new form.

Just a few moments after she began, Mira took her hands off the refining station.

"Wait! It's dangerous to remove your hands while refining...!" Toma panicked, but then he saw the swirling particles of light overflowing from the refining station and he stopped to gape in awe. The fading light revealed one large, clear stone sitting atop the station.

Toma couldn't believe his eyes. He brought his face close to the flawless stone to determine if his eyes were deceiving him.

"It's a Refining Stone... But how on earth did you make this so quickly?!" The entire process had taken less than a minute.

"I told you she was Danblf's pupil, did I not? She's learned all of his techniques," boasted Solomon, as though he'd completed the process himself. In all fairness, Mira hadn't learned any techniques because they had always been hers to begin with.

Technicalities aside, Mira affirmed his statement with a bored shrug.

"I mean, of course I knew that Master Danblf was a master of refining techniques, but I had no idea that his pupil would be just as skilled." Toma turned his attention to Mira. This girl... This *girl* might be the key to unleashing the maximum potential of the Accord Cannon. As he thought of the possibilities, he felt hope well up from deep within.

"Now then, Mira, so long as you're at it, could you join these into a pair of lightning-attuned Magic Stones?" Solomon added four more Magic Stones to the refining station.

With a *hmph*, Mira moved them into position and prepared to restart the process. Like before, it took less than a minute to create the shiny new Magic Stones.

"How's this?"

"Perfect." Solomon nodded with satisfaction as he picked one up. Unlike the faint glimmer of the natural Magic Stones, the refined materials shone with a strong inner light.

"I believe we have a solution for the Refining Stone and Magic Stone requirements," said Solomon as he handed the stones to Toma.

"Yes, sir!" Toma said with a smile, carefully cradling the ammunition in his palm.

As the room went back to discussing the Accord Cannon,

Mira took her robots back to a corner and resumed fiddling with them. But just as she started, one of the robed men approached her.

"Miss Mira, may I speak with you for a moment?"

"I'm busy. Come back later," she replied, fixating on the robots and refusing to looking away.

The robed man looked troubled as he crouched and begged. "Please, just a moment of your time."

Letting out a long sigh, Mira turned to the man. He was a handsome enough, wearing a blue and black robe with shoulder-length, shimmering blond hair. Surprisingly, he was someone Mira recognized.

"Wait...Cleos?"

"Oh! you've heard of me?"

This was the first time she'd met Cleos as Mira, but Danblf was well acquainted with him.

Cleos had been one of the researchers at the Tower of Evocation. His heritage was half light spirit and half elf. Since light spirits naturally illuminated the area around them, Danblf frequently brought Cleos along when he went adventuring in dark dungeons.

"Oh. Well, my master told me all about you." She'd been so surprised to see him that she blurted his name out without thinking. She decided to get back on script before she blew her cover.

Cleos gave a slight smile. "Ah, I see. Please allow me to properly introduce myself. I am Cleos, acting Elder for the Tower of Evocation."

"I'm Mira."

Pleasantries exchanged, Mira recalled the word *acting* in his introduction. Cleos was apparently the de facto leaders of the Tower of Evocation now.

"That's right. Graia did say that the towers were being served by acting Elders. I suppose that would be you."

"I was forced into the position, unfortunately." Cleos looked slightly embarrassed. "I spent so much time adventuring with Master Danblf that I was chosen by default. It's pretty much the same story for the others acting Elders."

"Hrmmm, you don't say."

It was a simple reason, but not the worst selection criteria she could think of. Cleos had been one of Danblf's strongest followers and was the only one who regularly accompanied him into life-or-death situations. At least it meant the acting Elders could hold their own, whether they enjoyed the job or not.

"By the way, is it all right for you to be missing this conversation?" Mira asked as she turned to look at Solomon and the others circled around the table. "This is an important weapon."

"It doesn't matter. The acting Elders are just here to fly the colors, so to speak. The important discussions are over; now they're just haggling over logistics and production. And that's the jurisdiction of King Solomon and the aristocrats."

"All of the mages present are the acting Elders, then?" Mira looked over at the robed mages lined up against the wall. Like Cleos, they each seemed to be amusing themselves in their own ways. "So what brings you to me?"

As Mira spoke, her eyes wandered back to the robots in her hand. She started turning them this way and that, trying to find out how they fit together once again.

The two drifted off into idle chitchat. Cleos kept finding ways to complain about how Danblf recklessly dragged him into dangerous places, and Mira forced a smile and nodded at appropriate times in the conversation.

She
Professed
Herself
Pupil of
the
Wise Man

16

UNABLE TO TAKE anymore criticism about her past self, Mira attempted to change the subject.

"By the way, are you still using that Thunder Tiger of yours?"

"Wait, Master Danblf mentioned my Thunder Tiger?" said Cleos with a surprised look.

"He sure did!" Mira decided to roll with the idea that her "master" had told her everything. It would mean less thinking about cover stories, less chance of slipping up, and more time to figure out how those dumb robots worked.

"Well, that's kind of embarrassing," said Cleos. "I'm surprised he talked about me at all." The idea that such an esteemed Wise Man took the time to tell his pupil so much about him brought a smile to his face.

"Oh, yeah. He told me all sorts of things."

"Well, my main summon is still my Thunder Tiger. But it's gotten a lot stronger compared to when I used to adventure with Master Danblf."

Stronger, eh? If I remember correctly, that thing was already pretty strong to begin with, thought Mira. "Ho ho. Sounds like a fine partner."

"Forging the summoning contract with the Thunder Tiger was such a pain. But then, Master Danblf, why he..." Complaints forgotten, Cleos moved on to speaking about how wonderful Danblf was.

Mira knew the truth. Danblf only brought Cleos along on adventures because the guy was a walking lantern. But as she heard his honest feelings about her former self and how much he felt that Danblf had taught him, she started to feel a touch of remorse for how poorly she'd treated him—even if he was just an NPC at the time. She tried not to let her guilt show by keeping her eyes on the toys in her hands.

"And now, fate finds me acting in Master Danblf's stead." With a satisfied look on his face, Cleos brought his tale to an end. There had been the occasional nostalgic moment for Mira, but most of it had been Cleos waxing on about Danblf's heroism. As the story finished, Mira decided to see what information she could get out of the acting Elder.

"By the way, I stopped in at the tower before I came to the palace. Compared to the Tower of Sorcery, the Tower of Evocation was practically deserted. Did something happen?"

Cleos's face—which had been bright and sunny—clouded over and threatened to rain. "You've hit on a...painful subject. Very few summoners remain."

"Hrmmm, as I feared."

Mira wondered at the time if it was just because she had visited so late at night, but Cleos's statement confirmed that things weren't going well. Summoners had never been the most popular class, and now their ranks had dwindled further. Her head sunk dejectedly, and she thought back to the days when the tower was a bustling hive of activity. Something had to be done.

"Mira, as Master Danblf's pupil, you probably forged your first summoning contract using the prescribed methods, right?" Cleos asked casually. As Mira had been lost in thought, he almost thought he caught a glimpse of Danblf in her manner.

Her first summoning contract—back then, it had meant loading your inventory down with restoratives and explosives. But she knew the method that Cleos was referring to was slightly different.

"You mean refined equipment and Blasting Stones," she said, referring to the more modern method devised and recommended by Danblf as Elder of the Tower of Evocation. The new method was intended to help those following in his footsteps. While it used crafted materials, it was more or less just a modernized version of the drug-and-bomb technique.

Instead of constantly topping off their HP with restoratives, the newbie summoner could up their endurance and durability stats with refined equipment; instead of using generic explosives, they used Blasting Stones with attributes that matched their target's weaknesses. The upgraded method made a world of difference when securing that critical first summoning contract.

"Just so! After Master Danblf disappeared, we were able to keep enrollment up for a while. But then the supply of Blasting Stones began to dwindle. Soon after that, the refining tools started to break down. Even the Palace refiners couldn't produce the same grade of materials. As time passed, the cost of materials rose, and their quality plummeted. Many prospective summoners were unable to beat the armor spirits and were either defeated or forced to flee."

"Ah... Hrmmm, I see."

Perhaps relying on a single person to subsidize the development program for an entire school of magic hadn't been the best decision. Add in a lack of charismatic leadership, and the result was that Tower of Evocation was on its way to becoming a ghost town.

"Right, well, let's start with this!" Done with her pondering, Mira opened her Item Box and withdrew all the Blasting Stones she had. After picking up the few that had fallen on the floor, she presented the lot to Cleos. "This should be enough to help about twenty people defeat their first spirit."

"Those Blasting Stones are as strong...no, *stronger* than the ones we used to have thirty years ago. Are you sure I can have these?" Cleos's eyes widened at the collection of brightly shining stones in Mira's hands.

"Of course. This is all I can do for now, but we'll work on the problem later."

"Master Danblf gave these to you for your protection, didn't he?" Cleos asked, concerned about Mira's welfare. Blasting Stones could serve as a powerful trump card in an emergency. They'd help the tower immensely, but Cleos could not accept them if they were going to cause Mira undue hardship.

"Don't worry about it. I have my Dark Knight for protection. I'm sure my master wouldn't stand for the tower's current state, either."

"That's true. Master Danblf was always crazy about the summoning program. I'm sure he'd try to right the ship," Cleos muttered to himself as he accepted the stones from Mira's out-stretched hands. "Thank you, Miss Mira. I'll contact the aspirants who gave up on summoning and tell them that they now have a reason to hope."

Cleos bowed to Mira as a wide smile spread across his face. He finally had the beginning of a solution for the Tower's problems. He'd tried so hard during the past thirty years, earning little more than frustration for all his efforts. The man deserved a turn of good fortune.

"Good idea. Do that. Oh, and take these as well." She decided to give him another parting gift to help reboot the recruitment effort. Slipping off one of her rings and a necklace, she strung them together and handed them to Cleos.

"This is too generous," he began, staring at them in awe.

"Those are specially made to boost strength and magic power. Together, they should allow a novice to stand up to any beginner-level guardian spirit."

"Are you certain you can part with something so valuable?"

"Of course. My master would want you to have them, and so

do I. But in return, I expect you to continue your stalwart stewardship of the tower. Thank you, Cleos."

"I swear it. On my name and my title as acting Elder, I shall rebuild our tower!" Cleos's spirit surged and his eyes shone with the power of resolve.

"All right, we'll conduct phase two of the experiment five days from now at the usual time." Solomon concluded the meeting. The nobles and acting Elders bowed and filed out of the development room.

"Looks like they're finished," observed Cleos. "Thank you for all you've done, Miss Mira. We'll start contacting people immediately. Things are about to get busy."

"Sure thing. Have a safe trip back."

Cleos gave a deep bow and left the development room, jogging to catch up with his peers. He was almost skipping, and the other acting Elders reacted with surprised looks and smiles. He was known for his fondness for children, and they thought he had simply enjoyed his conversation with Mira. They'd become accustomed to his dour disposition and this was the first time they'd seen him in such high spirits in a long, long time.

Only Mira, Solomon, Luminaria, and Toma remained in the conference room. Solomon pulled out a stack of documents from a back shelf and began to read through them with a knowing smirk.

Luminaria padded quietly behind Mira to peer over her shoulder. She'd made no headway on the toy robots.

"Are you still messing with those?" she grumbled, plopping down next to Mira.

"Aren't they cool? I've almost got them figured out!" Mira said with a look of childish joy on her face.

"Almost have what figured out?" Toma asked, filing papers away in his briefcase. He wandered over to Mira and saw what she was playing with. "Oh, that's my *Super Combiner Lord Vulcan*. Where'd you find that?"

"On the back of this shelf over here," Mira replied, pointing.

"So that's where it was hiding. I thought I'd lost it." Toma gazed at the jumble of robots in her hands with a nostalgic expression.

"Ho ho! So these were yours?"

"Yes. Well, actually, I created them."

"Oh, really now? You have good taste, sir."

"It was just a hobby...but it looks like I turned tinkering into a job. I was so excited to make those, but in the end, I screwed up the design. They don't fit together."

"I'm sorry...what was that?" Mira turned to stare at Toma, an expression of disbelief on her face.

He smiled apologetically. " Well...I made a slight mistake when I fabricated the combining mechanism. I needed to disassemble and rebuild it, so I put them aside for later... Then I forgot where I put them."

"You've got to be kidding me!!"

Her furious scream echoed beyond the confines of the development room as Mira transformed from an adorable girl into an avatar of rage. Toma stammered an excuse while slowly backing away, clutching the toys to his chest and promising to fix them before fleeing the room.

"Hah. Ha ha. Ha ha ha ha!"

A sinister laugh filled the space left in the room by the chief engineer. Mira turned, finding Solomon standing with a stack of papers in his hand.

"Finally! We can start full-scale development of the Type 10!" He spoke with lips bent in a creepy smile, staring straight at Mira.

"Oh, boy, here we go again." Luminaria saw the documents in his hand and his manic grin. Mira turned to ask her what she meant, but a moment later, Solomon was standing uncomfortably close.

"Up until now, we've been forced to focus on energy-saving designs," he said with an unsettling leer. "Our resource production couldn't keep up with demand. But now...*you're here.* We've got a practically unlimited supply of high-output Magic Stones. We can finally stop worrying about petty things like energy conservation. It's time to go all out—*it's time to get me that Type 10!*"

Mira realized that his grand vision would require the consumption of hundreds of Magic Stones. It would take six months to prepare that many—not exactly a practical idea. But Solomon was deep in his rant and could not be stopped.

"Technomancy is still in its developmental phases," he continued. "But I can see the potential. Just look at the increased output using mid-grade Magic Stones. It's incredible! If we can get high-grade stones, we can..."

For the next half hour, Solomon outlined his master plan to become the first kingdom on the continent to construct and field a tank battalion.

Mira's head lolled and she shook off a wave of drowsiness. After a long day of travel and fighting, an impromptu lecture about supply chain management wasn't the most stimulating evening entertainment.

"All right, that's enough for today," Luminaria cut Solomon off before he could shift into a higher gear. "Look at her; she's practically asleep on her feet."

"Fine..." Dropping the subject, Solomon went to return the papers to their place on the shelf. Even though he was denied an opportunity to continue his rant, he took solace in the fact that the answer to his biggest problems was falling asleep in front of him.

"Come on, you. Wake up." Luminaria poked Mira on the cheek.

"I'm not asleep." Mira slapped at Luminaria's hand and glowered at her. But the effect was somewhat lessened by the languid blink that followed.

"But you're tired, right?"

"Indeed."

"Have you had a bath yet?"

"I don't need one."

"Oh, no. No, no, no." Luminaria scooped Mira up and tossed

her over her shoulder. "You can't turn into a woman and then choose not to take a bath!"

Mira started to argue, but she was too tired to make the effort as Luminaria carried her from the room.

We've still got a pile of problems facing us, but at least we've got a fighting chance now, Solomon thought as he watched the two disappear, then casually made his way toward the men's bath.

"Why exactly do we need to bathe together?"

The scent of the bath tickled Mira's nose, pulling just a bit of the sleep from her eyes. She had to admit that the palace's massive bathhouse piqued her curiosity. It hadn't been here thirty years ago.

"Why not? The bath is large enough, and it's been forever since we last saw each other. Let's tear down those physical barriers and hang out for a while," Luminaria said while carrying Mira into the changing room.

Luminaria quickly stripped out of her clothes before folding and stacking them in a cubby. Mira, on the other hand, struggled with the ribbons that Lythalia and Mariana had used to secure her robes.

"Seriously? Here, let me help you." Luminaria began undoing the ribbons one by one with a practiced touch, putting her voluptuous figure on display right in front of Mira. She found a spot on the far wall to look at while Luminaria finished disrobing her.

Twenty ribbons were lined up on the shelf before the robe finally fell open, reverting to its original fit as Mariana's hair clip was removed. The collar gaped so wide that her shoulders were exposed, and Luminaria smirked as Mira's modest breasts peeked out from behind the edges of the open garment.

"I see everything is to your specifications."

"Please stop mentioning that..." Mira shuffled to a corner of the room where she pulled her arms through the sleeves and shrugged out of the robe.

Now that her magical girl-esque outer clothing was off, her undergarments were on full display. Luminaria leered at the Angel's Down Raiment and drawers, wiggling her eyebrows suggestively.

"Look at you, growing up so fast. Sheer lingerie and old-fashioned drawers? That's quite the juxtaposition."

Mira threw the robe at Luminaria's face and stripped before running into the bath. The sorceress carefully folded the discarded clothes and added them to the cubby next to hers before following along.

"This is madness! Solomon went all out!" exclaimed Mira as Luminaria entered the bathing area.

The bath was unabashedly luxurious, a showcase of the nation's decadent charms. The large walk-in basin was continuously filled by a fountain that sprayed hot water toward the ceiling. As the droplets rained back down, they transformed the surrounding area into an opulent shower.

Mira's drowsiness was washed away by the spectacle, and she giggled as she bathed under the fountain's warm cascade. Within no time, her hair had absorbed the water and was sticking to her skin. Little rivulets of water made their way down her body toward the floor. Mira kicked at the ankle-deep water in the shower area, enjoying every bit of the wonderful bath, which surpassed even the most glamourous spa back in Japan.

Luminaria hummed the theme song to an old familiar anime to herself as she soaked, in a state of total relaxation.

"She's really leaning into the whole small-and-cute thing. But is this really what you wanted, Danblf?" Luminaria muttered to herself as she watched the frolicking Mira.

After finding satisfaction in the pure waters of the bath, Mira returned to the changing room. Her robe and undies were gone— removed to be taken to the laundry. A change of clothes had been left in their place.

Mira picked up the garments, unfolded them, and froze. A frilly, sky-blue dress had been issued to her in place of her robe. Clearly, the maidservants had an opinion about Mira's ideal style. But her dismay at the dress was soon overshadowed by the terror that was hiding just beneath it.

Under the dress, she found...a little pair of white panties topped off with a tiny bow. They were nothing fancy, but somehow their simplicity made them far more intimidating than the drawers had been. Mira's life was complicated enough as it was without adding confrontations with undergarments to the list. These panties were just cute insult to adorable injury.

She rushed to open her Item Box, hoping to find an alternative. No escape from her predicament could be found within. Looking away from the underwear to regain her composure, she came face-to-face with a beautiful girl who would look very good wearing the panties.

"Huh...uh, a mirror."

Mira stared at her nude reflection, transfixed.

"I'm adorable," she muttered.

The first time she'd seen herself, it had been a distorted reflection in the luster of a knight's armor. Then her chamber window, tinted with the darkness of the night, had offered her a dim glimpse. But this was the first proper mirror she had encountered, and it fascinated her. There was no denying that she'd fulfilled all of her...*preferences*.

Mira dried herself with a towel as she stared into the mirror, before gently bringing a hand to her face. Her fingertips traced from her cheek to her lips, then down her neck, before reaching up to run through her bewitchingly long silver hair.

"One of us. One of us," chanted Luminaria quietly with a lecherous grin.

Mira, who had been completely lost in her own little world, jumped at the sound of the implication-laden voice. "How much did you see?"

"I came in to *'I'm adorable.'*"

Mira rushed forward using her Immortal Arts, Movement: Shrinking Earth. But Luminaria flickered like an illusion and effortlessly avoided the blow.

"What? That's new," Mira said, dumbfounded. She stared at the air where Luminaria used to be. Her curiosity about the new technique overwhelmed any anger she had felt a moment earlier.

"Technomancy isn't the only change since you've been gone. The march of progress never ceases."

Illusions of Luminaria began to flicker on and off all around the room. Mira was enthralled.

"This was developed around eight years ago. It's an evasion technique called Mirage Step. What it does is... Well, that's pretty obvious, right?" Images of her voluptuous nude figure popped in and out all over the changing room. "The only conditions are that you have the blessings of both light and water. And enough mana to make it work, of course."

"Oh! Then I should be able to learn it too! You gotta teach me!" Mira lunged at Luminaria, eager to learn, but the illusion flickered out like a dying hologram.

"Hmmm, should I? I dunno. It took so long to research..." Luminaria feigned reluctance in the face of Mira's insatiable appetite for skills.

"Hmph, fine. Be that way. I'm sure Solomon will teach me," Mira said as she threw the bath towel away. Luminaria flashed into existence, catching the towel and draping it over her hand like a stage magician's prop.

"Hmm, I wonder what I have here?" She pulled the towel off with a flourish, revealing a book in her hand: *Encyclopedia of Skills, 2146 Edition.*

"W-wait, is that...?"

The *Encyclopedia of Skills* was a perennially best-selling volume that collected all the countless abilities and techniques into one text. Of course, Mira had a copy in her Item Box—but that was the 2116 edition.

Her eyes were locked onto the book. Even during the four years after launch, skills were constantly being discovered and improved. But now? She knew the wisdom contained in the encyclopedia must be *immeasurable*.

"It's quite rare, and no amount of money will get you a copy in any bookstore on the continent. What if I told you I'd give it to you?"

"What are you after...?" Mira asked. To Luminaria, the book must be old news, but to Mira, it was irresistibly enticing. The sorceress wasn't going to hand it over for free; that much was obvious.

"Always the quick one! I'm not going to ask for much, nothing you can't handle. I heard from Solomon that you're going out to search for the others. I just need you to pick up a couple of things along the way."

"Ho ho! What items did you have in mind?"

"I need the Sword of the Crimson Lotus King and some Yggdrasil Charcoal."

"Hrmmm. Both are pretty rare. Not impossible to get, but probably annoying. I think it's doable. Clue me in, though—why do you need them?"

"I can't leave the kingdom. There's the whole thing with the Accord Cannon development. But mostly it's because Wise Men are considered walking weapon systems, all by ourselves. We can provoke other countries by simply crossing their borders. And I stand out a bit," Luminaria said, jiggling her breasts as she smiled broadly.

"Point taken, so you can knock that off. I suppose I will have a bit more freedom of movement—even if you could do with a little less."

"You understand perfectly. And in return for your services, you get the book." Luminaria waved the book in Mira's face as if showing off.

"Fine. But what are you going to do with the sword once you get it? You're not exactly a sword-and-shield sort of woman. And what do you need the charcoal for? I thought you didn't like dealing with alchemy because of all the fiddly details."

These were all valid questions. Luminaria was a top-class sorcerer, but the Sword of the Crimson Lotus King only reached its full potential when wielded by an advanced swordsman. And the only detail-oriented work she had ever shown interest in was making her avatar perfectly seductive.

"Well, I'm not going to be using them for their intended purposes. They'll just serve as catalysts." Luminaria lightly tapped the book she was holding against Mira's head as though it was a catalyst itself.

"A catalyst...to learn new spells? Go on." Mira looked up at her quizzically.

"Mmm-hmm. A few years ago, I saw a pentagram I'd never seen before, and after analyzing it, I found that I needed those two items to trigger it."

As Luminaria talked, Mira saw an opportunity and reached for the book above her head. But alas, the sorceress blinked back out of existence before popping back up a few feet away.

"These past thirty years must have been amazing," said Mira, spinning to look at her friend. "Wait, did you say *analyzing*? What's that? I thought you just tried whatever magic catalysts you could find until something worked. Does this analysis tell you the proper catalysts?"

"Yep. It's a new skill called..." Luminaria flipped through the encyclopedia looking for a certain page. "Technical Analysis. It was an evolutionary outgrowth of the appraisal skill. And it's in this book."

Luminaria dangled the tome in front of Mira, whose hand shot forward at lightning speed but passed through the illusion.

"Hrmmm."

"You've got a lot of catching up to do if you want to challenge me, sweetie. So how about it? You find what I'm after and I give you the book."

"Deal." Mira turned to Luminaria, who had used Mirage Step to flicker behind her, and added with a gleam in her eyes, "But I have one condition."

"Hmm? Travel expenses or necessary tools? I'm sure Solomon will provide those."

"No, I want an advance. Teach me that illusion technique." She looked up at Luminaria and batted her eyelashes. Even Luminaria was taken aback by the wanton display of cuteness.

"Oof, that's gonna be dangerous. Fine. Consider it a down payment."

And so began a naked study session in the changing room.

The lesson didn't take long. Once she knew the basic idea, Mira had no problem using the technique. But her roughness was evident when compared to the polished skills of Luminaria. Practice makes perfect, after all.

With the study session over, they went back to getting dressed. Luminaria turned while getting dressed and saw Mira standing there staring at the dress and panties in her hands. She'd and quickly grasped the situation.

"Are they really that bad? You might want to pick another hill to die on, because the War of Adorable Underpants has just started."

"But I..." Mira whined as she turned toward Luminaria. She froze, staring wide-eyed at the robes Luminaria was wearing. "Why do you get robes...?!"

"Because I come here all the time and keep spare clothes at the palace."

"Well, lend me one! I can't wear these."

"Nah. It'd be way too big for you. And hey, that'll look good on you. Don't worry about it." Luminaria had a lecherous smile as she leaned in toward Mira. "Do you need help putting them on?"

"No, thank you!" Mira used an illusion to escape to the other side of the dressing room. Sighing loudly, she resigned herself to the inevitable and shoved the dress over her head.

It was snug with her wet hair trapped inside. Reaching back and under the straps of the dress, she pulled her sparkling silver locks free.

All that was left now was the panties. Mira was torn—she could either go commando or throw away the last of her pride. On one hand, the dress was short enough that going without panties was a risky choice. On the other, the last of Danblf's dignity was hanging by a thread.

The dilemma was brought to a swift and anticlimactic end.

"Come on, just get it over with," muttered Luminaria as she snatched the panties from Mira's hand and crouched down by her feet. "Here we go now, leg up."

"No... But I..."

"Hurry up." Luminaria poked at Mira's foot. Reluctantly, Mira lifted her foot slightly, and Luminaria quickly slipped it through one side of the panties. "Now the other one."

Mira gave up. She lifted her other leg, and the panties slid into place over her hips.

It was a repeat of the drawers incident. But as she left the changing room, she felt some of Danblf's pride evaporate like the steam in the shower.

The guest rooms were located near the maids' quarters. After being led to her suite, Mira immediately crawled into bed.

What a crazy day, she thought, going back over everything that had happened. There was no doubt left—the game was now reality and she was stuck inside. But her friends were here.

She wasn't alone.

She Professed Herself Pupil of the Wise Man

17

A VIOLENT POUNDING on the door pulled Mira from her dream-filled slumber.

"Hnnngh..."

She looked around the luxurious room through squinted eyes for a bit before remembering where she was. Meanwhile, the banging at the door continued. Mira got out of bed to see what was going on.

Her sudden appearance at the door, clothes still disheveled from sleep, slightly dazed the guard, but he swiftly averted his gaze and gathered his bearings.

"Ah, good morning, Lady Mira. I bear a message from King Solomon. He asked that you be brought to him immediately. It's urgent."

The guard was breathing quite heavily. Behind him, the hallway was filled with people rushing about.

"Hrmmm, then let's be off." It was clear that whatever the situation was, it must be dire.

"Miss, perhaps you should get dressed first...?"

Mira had been just about to leave her room when the hesitant words of the guard stopped her in her tracks. Her nightgown left little to the imagination.

"Yes, I suppose so. What a bother," Mira huffed. She closed the door and quickly fixed her outfit, then headed off to the office where Solomon was waiting for her.

"Send the Second and Third Companies of the Magic-Clad Knights to the Southwest. In the Southeast, divide the Fifth Knights Corps into two divisions. I'll leave the formations up to you."

The palace was in an uproar. Solomon's voice echoed from the open door of his office, and the officer who'd received the order dashed from the room, narrowly avoiding a collision with Mira. She watched him sprint down the hall and then entered the office.

Solomon fell back into his desk chair, exhausted.

"What's going on?"

"Good morning! We have an emergency."

Solomon's head snapped back to attention, and he began tapping the map on his desk and waving her over impatiently. He usually didn't allow himself to get agitated, but he was clearly in a panic. Mira was far more interested in this rare occurrence than whatever might be the cause.

"That's what it looks like. What *kind* of emergency?"

"Two hours ago, we received a report that a horde of nearly three hundred monsters has appeared."

As he spoke, he pointed to an area on the map east of Lunatic Lake. It was too close to the capital for comfort...but three hundred goblins weren't worth turning the palace upside down. Mira began to feel a sliver of anxiety.

"Three days in a row is curious, but—"

Solomon cut her off with a gesture and pointed to another area of the map. "Fifteen minutes later, another horde of three hundred popped up here."

"What...?" Mira couldn't remember two swarms *ever* appearing at once. It also seemed to be a first for Solomon, given his reaction. But there was more.

"Thirty minutes ago, we had two more incursions reported— here and here. The first comprised of two hundred individuals, the second...*eight* hundred." With a sigh, he moved his finger again. "And just a moment ago, I received two more reports, each of those three hundred strong."

As Mira traced the path of his finger with her eyes, she raised an eyebrow, disturbed by what these anomalies might portend.

"And as if that weren't enough, the reports all mention a strange creature at the center of every horde. Based on description and the events of yesterday, I'm assuming they're all Lesser Demons."

"Hrmmm, so you're saying that all the incursions are being incited?"

"That would seem to be the case."

Solomon pulled his finger from the map and collapsed back into his chair. "There's also a flower field in the path of each horde. Those fields must hold some sort of significance."

He closed his eyes in thought.

"I wonder if they're going to kill each other again," pondered Mira aloud.

"A definite possibility." Sitting back up, Solomon pointed to the incursion in the southern reaches of the kingdom. "I've dispatched Luminaria to take care of the eight hundred monsters here. I need you to take the two hundred up in the north."

The horde that Solomon indicated was near the same flower garden that Mira visited the day prior.

"Two hundred, huh? That shouldn't be a problem, but are you sure you don't want me somewhere more...dangerous?" At Mira's jesting tone, Solomon gave her a bold smile.

"I think this might actually be one of the more difficult assignments," he announced bluntly.

Mira tensed and waited for the other shoe to drop.

"There aren't as many of them, but if we're right about the flower gardens playing some sort of critical role, then they're the closest to their target. We must strike quickly, but I'm not too worried; as you well know, I can arrange a fast ride."

An incredibly fast ride. Mira smiled bitterly as she realized what that meant.

"One other thing," Solomon continued. "Eyewitness reports said that the Lesser Demon in this horde is carrying a black, crystalline object."

"A black crystal...? You don't think they mean a Demon Crystal, do you?" Mira didn't like where this was going.

"I can only assume so. Which is why you're the one for the job."

"I see. Maybe it won't be as easy as I thought." Wishing she'd been tasked with putting down one of the larger swarms, Mira gave a strained laugh as she accepted the assignment.

"Good luck, One-Girl Army!" Solomon said with a wide smile.

With that encouragement still ringing in her ears, Mira made her way to the garage where preparations were under way. As she expected, the FAV was waiting with its engine idling.

Garrett popped out of the vehicle, a smile on his face as he bowed energetically. "Miss Mira! I'll be your driver again today."

"Ah...well, I'm in your capable hands, then."

"Looks like we're all here now. Let's head off." The armored rear door of the vehicle opened with a creak as he tugged on the handle.

"Hrmmm, so who else will be joining us today?" Mira climbed into the back of the car, finding two more occupants waiting for her.

"So the trump card King Solomon mentioned was you, Miss Mira? That does put me at ease." Joachim turned to smile at her warmly.

In contrast, the other passenger remained silent and disgruntled. Reynard was inspecting some nonexistent speck of dust in the corner of the passenger compartment to avoid making eye contact.

Not surprising, thought Mira. *But why are these two tagging along?* Mira took the seat next to Joachim as she tried to puzzle out Solomon's reasoning.

"Okay, here we go!" called Garrett from the driver's seat as he revved the engine. The slight morning fog that had been settling at the garage's entrance was immediately blown away as the FAV shot forward.

"He needs to go to driving school…" muttered Mira as the FAV flew down the cobblestone street.

"I'd heard the ride was rough, but this is more than I expected," Joachim said, trying to find a handhold to keep him from bouncing off the couch.

"Urgh…this has to be some sort of prank." Reynard's thick head hit the side of the compartment as a rear wheel struck a curb while taking a tight turn.

Forced to buddy up on the sofa, all three passengers grumbled their complaints as they tumbled and bounced.

As they headed to intercept the monsters, Mira and the other passengers discussed how best to deal with the horde.

"I'll take the front line. Joachim, you provide rear support as usual. As for you—" Reynard turned to Mira. He was at a loss for where she might fit into the order of battle.

"Miss Mira…" Reynard wore a serious expression. While he might not have been Mira's biggest fan, his tone made it clear that he was attempting to be respectful. "King Solomon commanded us to leave the Lesser Demon to you. But honestly, I'm unsure as to your strength and abilities. Will you be able to handle it on your own?"

"Of course. Even if we get a bad pull, it shouldn't be a problem."

"A...bad pull? What in the world does that...? Never mind. Just make sure it doesn't escape." Reynard returned to his trademark glare.

"Obviously. Try not to make any mistakes yourself." She snorted, then smirked and returned Reynard's glare with one of her own.

"Come now," Joachim said in a soothing voice, trying to calm and unify the party. "Miss Mira's abilities have been recognized by King Solomon himself, so I'm sure they're up to the task. But Miss Mira, I must ask you to have faith in us as well. Reynard may be brash, but he's also steadfast and tenacious. He will stop at nothing to protect his king and country. I cannot claim to be at the level of an acting Elder, but I have confidence in my magical abilities. I won't hold us back."

Reynard looked as if he were about to continue the argument, but instead, he just grunted "Of course." He turned his gaze to the windshield.

Mira had no doubts about Reynard's ability—otherwise Solomon wouldn't have chosen him to lead the King's Guard. She respected his loyalty and service to her best friend.

She would never in a million years tell Reynard that.

"I'm not worried." With that said, Mira also turned to look out the front windshield. Up ahead was the familiar sight of the grassland.

The FAV went barreling across the landscape, hitting every bump and ditch in its path. She reflexively lowered her posture and tucked herself deeper into the sofa.

Tall green grass surrounded the vehicle on all sides. She heard the swishing sound of the vegetation as it scraped against the armor plating. Though Garrett seemed to intentionally drive over every rock he could find, the magically reinforced frame kept the vehicle intact and undamaged. The occupants weren't so lucky. Unfortunately, Solomon's seat belt development program was lagging behind his weapon and armor research.

"Urgh...not this again," Reynard mumbled with a pained grimace.

"It is extremely fast, but it seems we need to do something to address the safety issues," said Joachim as he retook his seat after tumbling off the sofa.

"We might also need to replace the driver." Mira's prior experience had allowed her to properly brace herself for impact. She glared daggers into the back of Garrett's head, who seemed to be living for the adrenaline rush.

While it wasn't a smooth trip in any sense of the word, it was certainly fast.

As the FAV rolled toward its target, the communications system streamed in updates from the various watchtowers maintaining surveillance on the monstrous horde. It was without a doubt moving toward the same flower field where Mira and Garrett had been the previous day.

"Hrmmm...so we shouldn't kill them within the boundary of the flower fields." Joachim mulled over Mira's story from the day before.

"That's right," she said. "As soon as they arrived, they started killing each other. That must have been their goal, even if I don't know *why* it was their goal. And the Lesser Demon that instigated the whole thing was cackling as it died. It's conjecture, but I feel it wanted to die there as well."

"Their aim was to die in the flower field? A poetic end to be sure. But perhaps..." Joachim closed his eyes and mumbled to himself as he considered what Mira had said. He slowly opened them before making his guess. "That might be it. They could be trying to create an Undead Swamp."

"An Undead Swamp? Can those be created?" Mira was surprised by the suggestion.

Mira knew of them, though she had never experienced one firsthand. They were spawning points for undead monsters and were usually found in places associated with death—battlefields, execution sites, graveyards. In the game, they'd been popular sites for necromancy-oriented mages to farm materials.

"I've read some papers that hypothesized that they can be created, and the conditions they laid out have been met." Though Joachim was still unsure, no other reasonable explanation fit the circumstances. He explained what he could remember from his reading.

"First, the land itself needed to contain some sort of power. Then a large number of deaths must occur on the site. There were some other considerations listed in the treatise, but the central thesis was that a kind of transformative power is granted to a place through mass death. Even if the end goal isn't an Undead Swamp, the Lesser Demons are trying to warp the flower fields, regardless of whether we kill the horde ourselves or the demon triggers a mass suicide." As he spoke, his gaze was fixed on the rapidly approaching white pillar.

"Hrmmm, intriguing," Mira said. "No matter what the intent, if a Lesser Demon is involved, then I'm sure no good can come of it."

The power of death. It reminded Mira of occult legends she'd heard about back in her world, haunted locations and spiritual diseases. And in a world where demons and other fantasy creatures were a regular fact of life, those ideas were surprisingly easy to believe.

As she looked out blankly at the white pillar, her mind was filled with images of the flower field choked with the smoke from death pyres.

Or maybe they're trying to burn the kingdom down with a brushfire?

Mira's gaze passed across a small hill—the same one they'd bounced over yesterday. A moment later, the FAV accelerated, heading straight for it. At once, she knew what Garrett had in mind. She braced herself in her corner of the sofa and, noticing her preparations, Joachim did the same. Reynard paid no attention to the other two passengers; his eyes were fixed on the white pillar.

Suddenly, he was weightless. The windshield, which should have shown the pillar, displayed the blue sky for a moment before it filled with a sea of dark green grass.

"Urrgh! Not again!" Reynard shouted as the car landed hard on the ground.

It bounced and rattled, throwing him about. Mira and Joachim watched from where they were wedged into the sofa and heard the tortured sound of the FAV's suspension groaning as it landed. The mage breathed a sigh of relief that he was still in one piece.

As the shaking vehicle calmed back down, Mira looked out at the flower field ahead of them. There was the garden, but the monsters were still yet to be seen.

"Looks like we're getting there first," called Garrett from the driver's seat.

"If they're coming straight for it as was reported, they should emerge from the trees on the far right." Joachim surveyed the area and compared their current location to the one on the map, pointing to where the horde should be.

Sounding like a death rattle, a bitter voice echoed through the car. "Did you know that was going to happen? Why...why didn't you warn me?"

Mira and Joachim turned to see Reynard draped over the back of the sofa like a piece of dirty laundry.

"Ah, uh, sorry about that," apologized Mira. "I only realized what was coming just before it happened. I barely had time to brace myself."

"And I just saw what Miss Mira was doing and rushed to protect myself."

Though the words seemed reasonable, neither of them could fully mask their barely contained smiles and complete lack of remorse. Reynard's brow creased as he grimaced in pain. Then the FAV jolted as it hit something, and both mages tumbled off the sofa and onto the floorboards.

"You're the worst, Garrett..." muttered Mira as she climbed back into the seat.

"Indeed. Something must be done." Joachim smiled bitterly.

Reynard simply basked in their comeuppance.

18

"HOW IN THE WORLD...?" Mira looked at the flower field in surprise.

All about her, the flowers were blooming in a riot of color.

"Indeed, how strange," Garrett agreed.

Only yesterday a horde of monsters had rampaged through the garden, leaving the outer ring of flowers trampled and stained with their blood. There was no trace of the carnage. There were no scorch marks from the pyre of bodies Mira and Garrett had set alight, either.

"What is amiss?" asked Reynard as his eyes scanned across the beautiful garden.

"Not so much amiss as mysterious," Garrett said. "Yesterday's horde fought each other to the death in this field. Lots of carnage and collateral damage. But as you can see..." Garrett trailed off as his gaze returned to the field. "The flowers look lovely. No trace of blood anywhere."

The flowers swayed and rustled in the wind, the very picture of peace and serenity.

"I see what you mean," Reynard said.

"Mysterious indeed," murmured Joachim as he took another glance about the field.

Mira raised her head and looked out across the garden. Something else seemed different. In the center of the field, the white pillar stretched toward the heavens. Its top still shone a brilliant white, but the base was stained black as ink.

Mira stared at the pillar, trying to decide if it had changed or if she was just misremembering it. With all the chaos yesterday, she hadn't paid that much attention to it. If someone told her it had always been that way, she'd probably believe them. But a gut feeling told her that the black part was new.

Noticing the way her brow wrinkled, Garrett called out to her, "Miss Mira, what's wrong?"

"Does the pillar seem a little darker to you?"

"The pillar?" He narrowed his eyes and looked out toward the center of the field. "Now that you mention it, it does look that way...maybe. All I really remember from yesterday is the death and cleanup."

"Right? I can't tell if it's changed or not." She abandoned her attempts to remember and instead just gazed up toward the top of the pillar, where it grew hazy in the far distance.

Reynard had no interest in the pillar. As the others talked, he watched the surrounding forest for signs of the horde. He observed only the quiet rustling of branches and leaves blowing in the wind.

"The area is secure, but I wonder where those monsters are now," he said.

"According to the most recent report, they should be here soon." Garrett looked to the north-northeast, where the watchtower indicated the horde currently was.

"A little reconnaissance seems to be in order. That direction, right?" Joachim looked like he was preparing something.

"Correct. Assuming they continue straight ahead as reported, they should appear from behind those trees." Garrett indicated the spot with a wave of his hand.

Joachim put his left hand to his ear and pointed directly at the woods with his right. Mira watched with interest as Joachim's hands were enveloped in pale light.

Is that an Ethereal technique? she wondered.

A minute passed with no one daring to speak. Then Joachim released the stance, and his shoulders relaxed.

"So?" Reynard asked after a short pause.

"They're still a fair distance out. I could hear the footsteps of a group approaching this location—no doubt it's the swarm," Joachim replied as he stared into the forest.

"If we don't have to worry about them slipping in from another direction, then we should intercept them in the grasslands before they enter the woods," proposed Reynard, eyes fixed on the same location. "No point waiting for them to reach their target."

"Indeed. Let's make haste!" Garrett turned and ran back to the FAV. The other three followed slower, reluctant to reacquaint themselves with the vehicle's passenger compartment.

The FAV entered the edge of the forest, forcing Garrett to drive relatively slowly to avoid the trees. Mira took the opportunity to strike up a conversation once she had herself braced in the corner of the sofa.

"So Joachim, what sort of technique did you use to locate the monsters?" asked Mira.

"Ah, you mean the Art of Far Hearing?" replied Joachim as the car swayed gently from side to side.

"Ho ho! That's a new one. Is it classified as an Ethereal Art?"

"Indeed. It is an Ethereal technique, but it's classified as one of the Hidden Arts."

"A Hidden Art?" Mira's eyes sparkled at the tantalizing discovery. That was a phrase she hadn't heard before.

"Ah, that's right. You've been training with Master Danblf in seclusion, haven't you? I imagine you may be unfamiliar with many of the recent developments in techniques."

"Hrmmm, just so. Please go on." If Joachim chose to believe the rumors he heard, she was happy to play along. Mira made a mental note to let others supply their own assumptions more often when using her cover story.

"There are certain prerequisites needed to perform the Ethereal Arts, but the Hidden Arts require another layer of unique talents to use."

"Unique requirements? Such as?"

The car jolted, nearly throwing Mira off the side of the sofa, but she quickly resituated herself and gestured for him to continue. For Joachim, a fellow mage, her enthusiasm was entirely understandable.

"The truth is that those conditions are poorly understood. But it may have something to do with blessings from certain spirits, and the number and types of monsters the caster has defeated. The Art of Far Hearing is related to the blessings of Wind Spirits, but beyond that..." Joachim shrugged apologetically.

Then a sudden bump threw him forward, and he nearly struck his face against the bulkhead separating the passenger compartment from the driver's seat. After righting himself he continued, saying that the Ethereal Hidden Arts were incredibly difficult to learn and only a few people on the whole continent could use the Art of Far Hearing. He did his best to appear modest, but Mira detected an undercurrent of smug satisfaction by the end of his explanation.

"So I might not be able to learn the technique. Drat..." Mira sulked for a moment before the FAV jolted again, knocking her into Joachim's side.

"I'm definitely sending him back to driving school."

A few minutes later, the FAV emerged from the woods onto the grassy plain. They could see a writhing mass of bodies a kilometer to the north, drawing closer by the moment.

"Just where we thought they'd be. We'll face them here. Stop," Reynard ordered.

"Good lines of sight and no obstacles to interfere with spells. Perfect. Let's stop here," Joachim agreed.

"Indeed. No easy place for them to hide or escape. For the love of all that is holy, Garrett...please stop!" added Mira for good measure.

All three leaned forward and placed their hands on Garrett's right shoulder, head, and left shoulder individually.

"Understood!" Garrett gently applied the brake, bringing the vehicle to a standstill. Confirming that they had indeed stopped, the three let out a sigh of relief before disembarking.

"Good luck to all of you! I'll proceed to the rendezvous point as planned. Signal if you need me," Garrett said, pointing to a hill off to the right before checking that the doors were closed.

"Very well. I don't think we'll have a problem with a lot this size, though," grumbled the knight.

"Don't let your guard down, Reynard." Joachim gave his friend a gentle warning, more out of habit than out of concern.

"Hmph. You don't have to remind me."

Garrett hopped back into the driver's seat and fed another Magic Stone into the fuel box before rolling away. The FAV carefully made its way up the hill, moving slowly to avoid detection. Mira watched it with a cold look in her eyes, noticing that Garrett evidently *could* drive safely when he felt like it.

She voiced this opinion to her two comrades a moment later; Reynard and Joachim nodded silently in agreement.

"Right. Do you remember the plan?" Reynard called out to Mira as he switched into battle mode.

"Of course." Mira turned back to face the horde, tracing her chin with her finger. The pose would have held more weight if she still had Danblf's beard. Now it just made her look worried.

"They say Lesser Demons can use a strange form of summoning. Will you be able to handle that?" Joachim asked.

"Like I said before, I can handle any pull. No problem."

"Yes, you did say that. Well, if anything goes wrong, you'll have us here to help." At that, Reynard proudly took his shield in hand. Despite their earlier bickering, he was a professional and wasn't about to let personal feelings impact his duty. "Don't worry, and just focus on the horde."

"I'll leave the tanking to you."

Reynard heard her comment and let out a brief snort of laughter. Waving his sword in the general direction of the monsters, he calmly advanced while Joachim followed slightly behind. Mira split off, veering left. With luck and speed, she would flank the pack while Reynard and Joachim squared off against the front ranks.

At a distance, the swarm of monsters looked like a black wave crawling across the land, but as they grew closer, individual fiends were revealed. The horde was led by Dirty Hounds, four-legged monsters that raced across the plains. They were followed closely by Arch-Goblins, which had formed themselves into platoons.

In the center of the swarm, Mira caught a glimpse of the Lesser Demon.

Ugh. Why's it got to be right in the middle? she complained to herself silently as she moved to keep herself downwind.

Soon enough, Reynard and Joachim confronted the monstrous horde's front line.

Twenty meters of open grassland separated the knight from the swarm. Every time the wind blew, ripples spread across the tall grass that broke across the monsters like stones in a pond. They hesitated upon seeing Reynard—his intimidating presence was enough to make them waver.

Reynard readied his sword and the monsters stopped. It was two hundred against two, but their instincts told them that their path forward was blocked. The Dirty Hounds growled and glared. Reynard was undaunted; he took a step forward, followed by another.

Then the Lesser Demon in the center of the horde let out an ear-splitting screech. A squad of Dirty Hounds went berserk, snarling and barking as they fell upon the knight.

Mira could tell that Reynard lived for moments such as this. He stomped one foot forward, sending a shockwave through the air that sliced its way toward the horrors. The Dirty Hounds leaped forward and the shockwave engulfed them a second later. Reynard took another step, bellowing a battle cry as he brandished his sword.

The tip of his blade flashed through the air and came to a stop pointing at the sky. All sound vanished, and silence engulfed the area as even the wind lost its voice. Suddenly, the nearby grass shredded into tiny slivers, and a moment later, the attacking squad of monsters were all split in half and thudded to the ground, their dark blood staining the soil.

Niiice. Mira admired the long-range attack before shifting her gaze to the center of the horde.

Raising its hands in the air, the Lesser Demon screamed in rage and glared at Reynard. All the monsters in the horde milled about impatiently, awaiting their next command. The knight was a threat that must be eliminated.

At the demon's command, the horde changed formation. Reynard and Joachim held fast, waiting for them to approach. They knew the monsters' attention was solely focused on them. The horde encircled the pair, tightly packing themselves in and offering no chance for escape.

"Like we expected. Looks like we can continue our mission," Joachim whispered to Reynard.

"We're surrounded. Hostile targets in all directions. The situation is perfect." Reynard lifted his sword in a show of defiance, and the monsters roared in response.

The cacophony of impending battle filled the grassland, easily drowning out the sound of fast approaching footsteps. Only a sweet feminine scent drifting in from behind alerted the Lesser Demon that danger was approaching.

The Lesser Demon had placed itself as far away from its enemies as possible, while still leaving it in a position to observe and control its troops. But when it turned around, there was Mira. The commander of the horde found itself isolated and faced with the prospect of battling a child.

It's got a Demon Crystal. Just as I thought, it's a summoner.

When the Lesser Demon saw the two Dark Knights flanking Mira, it panicked and raised the black crystal in its hand toward the sky.

All right, let's see where this roulette wheel ends up, she thought with trepidation.

Unlike the summoning techniques that Mira used, the Demon Crystal summoned a magical beast at random. If Mira were lucky, it might be nothing more than another Dirty Hound. If she were unlucky, well...she didn't want to be unlucky.

Mira didn't try to interfere with the summoning; instead, she just stared at the magic circle spreading across the sky. It was usually easier to defeat summoning-type enemies before they could call in reinforcements, but Lesser Demons were an exception to the rule. Just before death, Lesser Demons released a black mist known as a Grudge State. It only lasted for a few seconds, but it cursed any magical item that came into contact with the cloud.

And if it touched an active Demon Crystal, the Grudge State's curse would start a chain reaction and force the crystal to automatically summon a top-tier beast. There was a chance that one of those would show up anyway, but the odds were low.

She waited patiently for the summoning to finish, letting out a little sigh of boredom.

The Demon Crystal began to glow with an eerie light, and the moment of truth drew near as the magic circle descended and expanded. Two legs, thick and crooked like old tree trunks, slammed into the earth.

"Hrmmm...*unlucky*," Mira muttered with a sigh. She recognized the legs.

They were followed by a tail that slowly stretched out and thudded against the ground. It was thick and covered with dragon-like scales. Finally, the rest of the beast emerged and the circle made its way skyward once more. Standing taller than the nearby trees, the creature turned its head as it checked its surroundings.

The magic circle fizzled out and the Lesser Demon, sure of its impending victory, let out a deafening cackle. A moment later, the beast's roar ripped through the air, drowning out the demon's laughter.

Reynard and Joachim frowned at the noise. Beyond the encircling horde of monsters, they saw a beast with the upper half of a rooster and the lower half of a lizard. It was a cockatrice, and any who met its gaze would be petrified—trapped forever in a nightmare of stone.

"That's too much for the girl to handle! We have to assist, Joachim!" A reasonable assessment, but the monsters surrounding the pair blocked any route to Mira's position. "Bastards! Get out of my way!"

"Calm yourself and look again," said Joachim, tapping him on the shoulder. "Miss Mira shows no fear before the beast. She can handle it, even if the situation seems dire."

Reynard was reminded of the cute, confident, and *annoying* smile worn by Mira when she assured them of her capabilities. The next moment, a pained scream rang out across the battlefield. As he watched and listened, he felt his anxiety fade away.

"Ah, right. She can handle it," he muttered, his voice suddenly calm as he turned and cut down a Dirty Hound that had taken the opportunity to lunge at him.

A few moments before, the cockatrice had landed on the ground. It spread its wings in a display of dominance and screeched to announce its presence. Red eyes scanned the battlefield and found a young lady to lock in its petrifying gaze. But before it could use its stare on her, half its vision suddenly went dark.

The cockatrice screamed in pain as blood flowed from the side of its face.

One of Mira's minions returned to her side. The Dark Knight held a sword freshly painted with blood, red drops cascading to the ground. Her opponent's ability to petrify depended on having *both* eyes locked on the target. This wasn't Mira's first cockatrice fight, even if it was the first time she'd fought one in a dress.

Despite losing its most powerful ability, the beast was still itching for a fight and screeched in indignation. The Lesser Demon was less confident. It was clearly unnerved by the sudden reversal of fortune and glared at the Dark Knights with fear in its eyes.

As Mira positioned her summons to finish the fight, the Lesser Demon screamed in an unknown language. As its remaining eye grew dull and docile, the cockatrice lowered its body, and the demon jumped atop the monster.

"Wh-what the hell...?"

Turning toward the white pillar, the cockatrice leaped into the air, bowling over friend and foe alike with the wind from its huge wingbeats. It flapped to gain altitude before making a gliding descent and awkward landing, more of a long jump than sustained flight. Mira stared after it in stunned disbelief, taken aback by the absurd retreat.

"Hey! Get back here!"

Mira took off after the beast as it plunged into the woods.

19

"CRAFTY BUGGER, aren't you?"

Her foes had fled the scene just as the battle was beginning, leaving her to give chase. It was close, but she finally overtook them just short of the flower field. With speed enchantments on her equipment and the dense woods hindering the movement of the cockatrice, Mira managed to place herself between the Lesser Demon and its intended destination.

Exhausted but resolute, she summoned three additional Dark Knights. Together, the young woman and five armor spirits surrounded the wounded beast and its demonic rider.

The Lesser Demon glared in irritation at the intimidating ghost-like beings. It had been sure that the cockatrice would escape easily, but now the opposition was back in greater numbers. Its getaway plan might have been foiled, but it wasn't giving up.

Pointing at Mira, the demon screamed, and the cockatrice charged with madness boiling in its eyes. Claws tore at the earth, sending chunks of soil and thick grass flying into the air. It might have lost the contest of speed, but it surely wouldn't lose a contest of sheer mass.

But the razor-sharp talons and gnashing beak never reached Mira. With a pitiful screech, the cockatrice crashed into the earth.

Mira's Dark Knights went to work the moment the creature lunged. Unsure of the creature's defenses, she had commanded her minions to work as a team and focus their attacks on the creature's right leg. They cut through the tough scales before mercilessly slicing the tendon and muscle tissue underneath. It worked, and now the cockatrice's charging days were over.

The beast struggled to its feet, limping and dragging its right leg behind it as it tried to withdraw from battle. But its rider had vanished.

Mira panicked, turning this way and that looking for her foe. Then, at the edge of her vision, she saw the Lesser Demon make a break for the field of flowers. The vile creature flashed out from behind a stand of trees and sprinted for its target.

Ho ho! Using a decoy, eh?

The demon was just a few meters away from the field now. Confident that it had achieved its goal, it turned and taunted Mira with impish delight. The foul creature threw back its head and cackled madly with victorious glee.

Mira didn't budge; there was no need. A gust of wind rushed through the grassland's edge. A gust of—roaring, jet-black fury.

The cackling suddenly cut off, and a hateful cry echoed through the meadow. It lasted only a split second before fading away.

At the terminal point of the gust of wind lay the corpse of the Lesser Demon, cleaved in two. Its face was distorted with rage and confusion as it stared into the sky with hollow, empty eyes. A few meters away stood a Dark Knight, a blood-soaked blade gripped in its fist.

Mira knew the demon's target was the field of flowers. She might not know *why*, but she knew that the only thing that mattered was preventing the demon from reaching the circle. So before the battle even began, Mira had issued the knights a general order to deny their foes' entry into the garden at all costs. The spirit had done its duty flawlessly.

The Dark Knight came back to Mira's side with a measured stride, as though nothing had happened. A black mist rose into the air; the Grudge State floated above the abandoned corpse. Something was amiss...

"Hmm, what?"

It should have just melted into the wind and dispersed. Instead, it began to move like it had a will of its own. Mira was perplexed and left three knights to face the wounded cockatrice while she carefully watched the mist's movements.

It approached, slowly but surely. It passed by the Dark Knight who had slain it and continued past Mira as well.

What is this phenomenon? Do they search for something to curse now? Mira traced her chin with her finger and looked on with a furrowed brow.

There was no wind in the meadow, and only the footsteps of her knight could be heard. Then, a groaning, wheezing sound echoed in her ears; the maimed cockatrice was growing restless.

Wait, it's going to curse...that? Mira looked to the beast, its eyes boiling with rage as it lay waiting for the black mist arrive.

If it moved even an inch, the Dark Knights would tear into it. But it kept still, discipline keeping a lid on the simmering rage and pain that threatened to drive it mad. It tamped down its urge to fight, silently following the Lesser Demon's final instruction.

The Grudge State suddenly swelled and accelerated as though being sucked in by the cockatrice, invading its body through its wounds, its eyes, and its beak.

The change was dramatic. The creature bloated, swelling dangerously like a bomb on the verge of exploding. It screeched—its voice was pitiful and filled with anguish. Flesh rose to knit scars across its wounds, and its remaining eye glowed with the promise of vengeance. Mira eyed the cockatrice warily as it grew to twice... no, three times the size it had been.

Finally, the mist vanished and the curse was complete.

The Grudge State should have only been able to curse an enchanted item, thought Mira as she observed the situation warily. *Is this another consequence of the game world becoming reality?*

As though it lacked control over its new body, the cockatrice looked around blankly, haphazardly spreading its wings and trembling. It seemed more disoriented and pathetic than dangerous.

"Oh, well, time to put you out of your misery." Mira sighed as she looked at the swollen cockatrice.

The three spirits surrounding it turned into a jet-black gale as they attacked the monster. Blades attacked its feet, wings, and body but failed to pierce the tough outer layer. What should have caused gaping wounds barely scratched the surface of the creature's hide. To make matters worse, the shallow wounds quickly healed, leaving only faint scars behind.

Hrmmm, it's definitely tougher than it was.

The Dark Knights were undeterred. Their swords moved faster, leaving deeper tracks in their wakes. Finally, after many repeated slashes, they sliced deep into the creature's flesh.

The cockatrice snapped out of its daze and glared at the summons with a bloodshot eye.

Its wildly flapping wings beat the air in an attempt to ward off the persistent assault, and a torrent of wind erupted from the creature. Trees creaked. Leaves scattered and flew skyward, and the nearby grassland rolled violently like waves on a stormy sea. Mira's light body was picked up and sent flying.

Moments later, the storm stilled and everything fell back to the earth.

"Ho ho! You seem a bit stronger." Kicking at the air like she was descending a flight of stairs, Mira landed safely on the ground.

The Dark Knights also regained their footing and surged back to their positions surrounding the cockatrice. The beast stared at the knight before it, the sight of the blade in its hand igniting the creature's rage once more.

Its beak gaped wide, and a screech erupted that split the sky like a clap of thunder. Mira's eardrums quivered hard and went numb before she could press her palms to the side of her head at the sound. She took half a step back and scowled.

"Tell me how you really feel, you big jerk!" Her annoyed muttering was lost in the metallic clank of the Dark Knights rejoining the battle.

Screaming in a frenzy, the cockatrice used its entire body as a deadly weapon. It slammed its bulk down on the spirits buzzing around it like so many biting flies. The Dark Knights remained relentless, their swords flashing as they parried, attacked, and dodged. The ferocious onslaught destroyed everything in its path, rending the earth and piercing the air, and the creature's hide somehow grew even tougher, blocking the blades of the Dark Knights.

Mira stood at a safe distance, observing. A single blow from the monster would be undeniably powerful. If it managed to land a hit on her, she probably wouldn't survive. ·

But...that was it.

There were no signs of the nasty magical abilities that the cockatrice originally possessed. Gone were its cunning and finesse. Now it was just stupidly swinging haymakers with all its might, like someone took a legendary spear and stuck a big lump of iron on the end. Its only advantage was the added toughness that resisted the swords of her Dark Knights—but they were slowly making headway, and it was only a matter of time before the massive creature fell.

Mira watched the battle with a troubled expression. Her victory was inevitable, but the sun would set before the fight ended at the current pace. Adding more Dark Knights to the equation might solve that problem, but she wasn't certain that she could maintain the same level of control with more of them on the battlefield. Additional summons could yield diminishing returns.

There was no need to hurry, she decided. It was best to hold her experiments until she could take the time to do them in a controlled environment. For now, she would simply observe so she could make an informed hypothesis later. Everything would be done by the book.

However, lying next to the body of the Lesser Demon...

Oh ho? What's this? Mira spotted a strangely glowing crystal out of the corner of her eye. Curiosity piqued, she walked over and picked it up. It was foul, and a tainted glow pulsed from within—the Demon Crystal.

This was new. In the game, the crystals had disappeared upon the demon's death. They were a visual-only part of the Lesser Demons' character model that players could not acquire.

"Oooh...! Ho ho ho. Now this is *very* interesting." An evil smirk spread across her face.

Defeated monsters no longer disappeared in a puff of pixels. They remained as corpses, eventually decomposing and returning to nature. This new cycle of death and rebirth had brought her an unexpected boon. Mira had long been intrigued by the possibility of using a Demon Crystal as a catalyst during their summoning rituals, and now she finally had one.

As Mira observed the crystal, the violent sound of two objects colliding rang out and a black blur flew past her. One of her

Dark Knights slammed into the soil of the garden, leaving a long furrow in the flowers before finally coming to a halt with its lower half buried in the ground. A moment later, it pulled itself free with inhuman ease and sprinted back to the battle.

Mira ignored the fight and went back to considering her newfound prize.

It looks just like an attribute crystal...but the color is different. Dark Attuned Crystals don't have such a sickening glow.

Attribute Crystals were versatile materials with applications in many fields, but they were intricately linked to the art of summoning. Summoners had an ability called Elemental Shift, which could be used to imbue a summoned spirit with an elemental attribute if the proper catalyst was available at the time of casting.

Mira pursed her lips and turned to look at the fight in progress.

"Why not? Just for kicks."

The meadow reverberated with the sounds of the cockatrice's screech and the clanging of the Dark Knight's swords. The grass beneath the battle was entirely destroyed, and the smell of spilled blood hung heavy in the air.

Mira stared at the open space between her and the battle and held the Demon Crystal aloft.

[Evocation: Elemental Shift Dark Knight]

As Mira released the power hidden within the crystal, she immediately noticed that the sensation of magical flow was different from when she summoned a Dark Knight. The magic circle expanded threefold as it absorbed the power from the crystal.

"I hope this was a good idea!" Mira wore a grin of excitement and terror on her face.

In the blink of an eye, the circle transmogrified into a mockery of its usual form. The odious magic began to writhe and squirm like a pile of maggots. Mira hustled away from the scene of the crime, sure that something had gone terribly awry.

Swelling like a clogged cyst, the magic circle erupted in a geyser that rained tainted blood down in all directions. The scene was spectacular and wretched. As the blood stopped falling, it revealed something huge filling the space.

It was a grand sight. The spirit wore the armor of a knight over the robust body of a beast. Unnaturally black, as though born from darkness, its eyes shone like blood-coated headlamps. It bore no sword. Instead, it possessed a mouth that split open to reveal countless sawtooth fangs.

"Astounding! I suppose I should call this a Dark…Beast?" At first glance, it appeared almost nothing like her Dark Knights, but as she studied it, Mira could see similarities. The Elemental Shift Summon resulted in a beast with a body like a large predatory cat shoved into a twisted pastiche of the Dark Knight's armor. Its appearance was grotesque, and it looked like it might start a rampage at any moment. Hungry eyes flicked about in search of prey as it walked to take its place obediently at Mira's side.

"That's a good sign, at least," Mira decided.

The battle between the cockatrice and the Dark Knights was less damaging to the combatants than it was to the surrounding area. It wasn't quite a stalemate—but it was a slow contest of the knights' agility and tenacity versus the colossal, regenerating mass of the cockatrice. The local forest was collateral damage.

"Time to wrap this up. All right, let's see what you can do." Mira told the Dark Beast. As she surveyed the battle, she waited for an appropriate opening before withdrawing her three Dark Knights.

The rampaging cockatrice charged blindly toward the new enemy. Carried forward by raw spite, its tree-trunk legs pounded the earth as its mighty frame bore down on the Dark Beast. A heavy metallic clang rang out and echoed through the ground, followed by a scream of spite tearing from the cockatrice's beak.

The Dark Beast caught the full brunt of the cursed creature's charge. The cockatrice bent its neck to snap at Mira's minion, which bellowed in return. The Dark Beast lunged, howling as its gaping maw bit and tore into the cockatrice's flesh. In pain, the dragon-like tail of the cockatrice thrashed against the ground again and again, sending thunderclaps through the air and tremors through the ground.

As she had with the Dark Knights, Mira issued orders to the Dark Beast as the battle progressed. Unlike her knights, it disregarded her commands and kept brawling.

Hmm, this isn't a summon for subtlety... It seems to have two settings: wait and attack, thought Mira. *A proper rampage is useful every now and then, but I'll have to find a way to put the brakes on this.*

Mira watched the battle play out with admiration and horror. "So...what's all this, then?"

"Hmm? Ah, Reynard." Mira turned at the sound of a voice and found Reynard and Joachim standing beside her. The two were watching the bloodbath with slightly pinched faces.

"I believe that one of the two titans is the cockatrice, even though it looks quite a bit different than I remember. The other one, however..." Joachim calmly tried to make sense of the situation.

Neither the Dark Beast nor the cockatrice would yield. Fang for fang, claw for claw, roar for roar they went at it. As the blood flowed freely, the battle did not wane but instead gained intensity. The two combatants were berserk with rage and pain.

"Ah, ahem. That would be one of my summons." Not knowing how else to describe it, Mira opted to shrug instead.

The three gawked at the spectacle like it was the dramatic finale of a *kaiju* film. Woodland creatures had long since fled the area, and the only thing left was the show.

"By the way, where's Garrett?" Mira asked, attempting to change the topic.

"We asked him to deal with the monster corpses. Normally, I'd immolate them myself, but he said that he'd take care of it. He seemed to be worried about you, but it looks like you have the situation...perhaps 'under control' isn't the right phrase, but..." Joachim responded as he watched the rampaging monsters with a glassy expression.

On the far side of the battlefield, they could see a red light stretching into the sky—a pillar of fire burning with incredible intensity.

Garrett wasn't worried about me at all, was he?

Mira imagined the expression on Garrett's face as he pulled the trigger for the FAV's fire cannon. It must have been brighter than the flame in the sky. After a few minutes, the cremation process concluded and the pillar of fire dejectedly sputtered out.

The sky filled with red again, except this time it was the blood of the cockatrice spraying upward from a gaping wound. The Dark Beast had managed to catch the mutated creature's wing in its wicked jaws before wrenching the feathered limb off at the shoulder. The cockatrice let forth another ear-splitting scream and thrashed in agony.

"...Brutal." The word slipped unbidden from Reynard's mouth. He considered the savagery playing out before them and reevaluated his assessment of Mira.

The Dark Beast opened its mouth and spat out the severed wing. Bright red blood poured from between its fangs before it turned back to its foe.

But the cockatrice refused to give in. Its remaining eye hadn't lost its fighting spirit, nor had the injury diminished its rage. It attempted to ward off follow-up attacks by thrashing its remaining wing, but the massive creature was unable to maintain balance. This was the opening that the Dark Beast had been waiting for.

Planting its four legs on the ground, the colossal minion opened its mouth as if to roar. A flickering, piercing light formed in the back of its throat, growing in intensity.

"Such magic power!" Joachim's eyes widened as he watched in awe.

But just before the Beast could fix its aim, the crippled cockatrice gave a mighty swing of its scaled tail. The blow landed on the side of its opponent's face; there was a dull thud and the Dark Beast's body shook violently.

It wasn't enough to stop the magical attack. The Dark Beast emitted a dazzling beam of light from its mouth, arcing through the air and unleashing the roar of a sonic boom. The tail strike had forcibly shifted the Dark Beast's aim, and the cockatrice avoided a direct hit. Instead, the light tore through the trees and gouged a deep trench in the rich forest floor. A secondary explosion of dirt and roots flew skyward as the beam dissipated.

The roar of the cockatrice faltered, its massive body collapsing to the ground with a violent crash. Though it had spoiled the Dark Beast's aim for a true kill shot, the cockatrice didn't emerge unscathed. Its left leg below the knee had been completely burned away.

"Looks like it's done for," observed Reynard with a hint of relief creeping across his face. Even at the bitter end, the battle continued without intervention from the three spectators.

The cockatrice still had a glint in its eye as it lay on the ground, but with only one wing and one leg, there was no way it could continue in any meaningful sense. It thrashed and snapped, waiting for the Dark Beast to sink sawblade-edged fangs into its writhing neck and bring its suffering to an end.

The Dark Beast had other plans. It reset all four legs and opened its mouth wide.

"Is it going to fire another blast?!" Joachim panicked, looking to Mira as if she had gone mad. She couldn't bring herself to make eye contact—she might have summoned it, but the beast refused to answer to any commands. It was acting entirely of its own volition.

"This one looks bigger than the last one." Reynard's statement drew their attention back to the beast.

Its first shot had charged for only two or three seconds, but now over ten seconds had elapsed. The light of the charging beam was growing far brighter than before. It was like the beast held a star in its mouth and threatened to unleash a supernova.

The image of the entire area being turned into scorched earth flashed through Mira's mind. From the look on Joachim's face, she was sure he was having similar apocalyptic visions. She had to act fast.

A moment later, a large magic circle appeared underneath Dark Beast. It had the same ominous, corrupted glow as when the beast was summoned, but now it dragged the creature in the opposite direction, howling in indignation as it departed.

The three waited with bated breath as Mira's banishment took effect.

But as the pulsating magic circle swallowed the Dark Beast, it still struggled to fight. Its entire body had sunk into the circle, but it managed to keep its head above the portal and the glow in its mouth suddenly grew brighter.

"Miss Mira!"

"On it!" Even as she spoke, Mira was already giving orders to her Dark Knights standing at attention nearby.

Moving as one, they smashed into the bottom of the Dark Beast's chin. A brilliant flash of light soared into the sky, penetrating high into the atmosphere, where it eventually dissipated into particles of light that rained down over the countryside. The banishment of the beast had finished, leaving no trace behind.

After a sigh of relief, the three shifted their gaze to the dismembered cockatrice. It groaned and tried to stand on its remaining foot, the wound below the left knee already sealed by a thick scar. It screeched in rage, still lost to the Lesser Demon's madness.

"Even though it's wounded, we can't let our guard down." Reynard said, squaring off against the creature warily.

"Indeed," agreed Joachim as he moved to support his partner.

"Stand down. This is still my responsibility." Mira put up a hand to still the other two while turning her gaze wholly to the cockatrice. Twenty Dark Knights appeared, surrounding it in the blink of an eye.

Reynard and Joachim were both taken aback by the sudden appearance of the spirits. None of the summoners in service to the army—not even Cleos—could create so many so quickly. The knight and mage had to acknowledge that the title of Wise Man's Pupil was no boast. If anything, Miss Mira might have been far too modest.

Despite its demonic powers, the cockatrice swiftly collapsed to the ground again. The Dark Knights fell upon it, wounding the pitiful monster over and over. Eventually, the assault overwhelmed its latent regeneration and blood spurted from innumerable wounds. The beast fell silent.

CHAPTER 19

The rain of light from the Dark Beast's particle weapon began to fall as the cockatrice was finally slain. Turning away from the grisly scene, Mira could see the droplets of shining magic twinkling in the field of colorful flowers. As they got caught by the wind and carried aloft, they sparkled and whispered like countless tiny angels.

Before her, Heaven. Behind her, Hell. Reynard and Joachim, caught between the two, silently turned to face Heaven as well.

JOACHIM HAD JUST FINISHED cremating the corpses of the cockatrice and the Lesser Demon when the FAV pulled to a stop nearby. Garrett exited the vehicle with an obvious look of disappointment on his face; he'd been hoping for an excuse to use the FAV's turret again.

With the mission completed and nothing left to do at the battle site, the team loaded back into the armored car and drove back to the palace.

It was a cheerful ride home, despite the bumps in the road.

Once again, Mira found herself lounging on the office sofa while picking at a snack. Solomon looked over the written report that Joachim had prepared as he listened to Mira's subjective account, asking the occasional question to fill the gaps.

"So the Lesser Demon cursed the cockatrice? In the thirty years I've been here, I've never heard of that happening.

Then again, it's been ten years since we've last seen a Lesser Demon."

"That long?" Mira raised her eyebrows. "To tell the truth, I was expecting the Grudge State to just fizzle out like usual. It was a bit more than I bargained for."

This world was so familiar, and yet so different—Mira could take nothing for granted. Something new to her might be commonplace, or it might be rare enough to surprise Solomon after three decades living here.

"Well, thanks for doing the heavy lifting," Solomon said, stacking the report on top of a pile of other reports. "These Lesser Demons... I wish we knew where they were coming from."

"Indeed. They're always bad news."

"That's the truth. We need to find their base of operations before things spiral out of control." Solomon signed and leaned back in his chair.

"Hrmmm, a base of operations..." Mira nibbled a cookie as she lost herself in thought, but as she sipped some tea to wash it down, inspiration struck. "Oh, wait, what was the name of that guy...?"

"Oh yeah...*that guy*. Thanks. That really narrows it down," Solomon said sarcastically. Mira was still terrible with names, and even if it was annoying, it made him a little nostalgic.

"You know. That NPC demonologist who was always chasing after Lesser Demons. He carried around all that holy water." She could remember his face. Bunching her eyebrows and pursing her lips, she struggled to remember his name.

"Oh, you mean Howard."

"Yes! Exactly!" Mira waved her half-eaten cookie at him and nodded in agreement.

Howard had been doing research on demons. He was a brilliant but absentminded older gentleman with a habit of brewing medicinal tea with holy water and offering it to everyone he came across.

"Hmm, I'm fairly sure he passed away a few years ago. He was already an old man back then, after all."

"Oh, that's a shame. I thought he might know something about this." Stymied, she shoved another cookie into her mouth while she thought of a work-around. "Well, if he's dead, what about using that other thing? Wasn't there some mirror that lets you talk to the departed?"

"The Mirror of Darkness, and stop talking with your mouth full. But that requires you to have a strong bond with the person in question or a powerful memento."

"Dammit. I don't think doing a couple quests with the guy counts as a strong bond." Mira sulked and sipped tea as she let her mind wander. "Speaking of which, wasn't there a whole quest about the mirror being cursed?"

"Right, there was! I think I met Howard on that quest."

"Yeah, he just popped out of nowhere and doused you with holy water."

"Oh! I almost forgot!" Solomon shouted. While the urge to slip into reminiscing was strong, Solomon still had the troubles of the kingdom on his mind.

"What's the matter?" Mira asked, bolting up from the couch.

"Luminaria interrupted us, but yesterday afternoon, we were talking about finding the rest of the Wise Men."

"Indeed. We were discussing who to look for and how to find them." Mira poured herself a new cup of tea before removing her shoes and stretching out on the sofa, preparing herself for an extended brainstorming session. "So I should go out and look for them, but do we know where to start? I need some clues to work with."

The Nine Wise Men were a strange collection of people. They could be anywhere, following their own flights of fancy with no one the wiser. How could she find people like that? As Mira swirled her teacup, she decided to leave that question to Solomon, using her recent arrival as an excuse.

"The Mirror of Darkness. That's what reminded me of this. Do you remember where the mirror was located?"

From what she remembered, the Mirror of Darkness was located in the basement of some undead-infested temple. A name surfaced in her mind.

"Soul Howl."

"Exactly. He's the only one of you Wise Men whose location should be easy to predict."

The Mirror of Darkness lay within the depths of the Ancient Temple Nebrapolis, simply called "the catacombs" by most players. Soul Howl, the Great Wall, Elder of the Tower of Necromancy, was morbidly obsessed with undead girls. It seemed obvious that they'd find him there, especially since Soul

Howl had once described the catacombs as a paradise. He was online but not in his tower, so it was probably worth checking to see if he was there.

"And if you're going there anyway, you might as well see if you can talk with Howard."

"Hrmmm, then I'd better bring some holy water with me."

"Good idea. My god, he loved that stuff." Solomon laughed.

"But the catacombs are pretty far from here. Wish I could use my Floating Island."

"I'll leave you to deal with travel... No, come to think of it, I can provide some help after all. But since this is a top-secret mission, we can't use the Pegasus Carriage or the Caravan."

"The Pegasus Carriage? Caravan? What are you talking about?"

"Ah, the Pegasus Carriage is what carried you here from Silverhorn. Pretty fast, wasn't it? It uses enchanted harnesses to drastically reduce the burden on the horses. Fastest carriage in the kingdom," boasted Solomon with pride, a big smile on his face.

"It was pretty quick. Not as fast as my Floating Island, though."

"Well, those aren't coming back, so get over it. Floating Islands were OP, anyway."

Mira signed with frustration. The Floating Islands had been nearly as fast as airplanes. Not even the FAV, the pinnacle of technomancy, could hold a candle to their speed and utility. They didn't need to consume a steady diet of Magic Stones to stay running, either.

"Anyway," Solomon continued, "Caravans are more about comfort, not speed. They're for extended trips away from the capital. I guess you could compare them to RVs."

"Ho ho. That sounds nice!" Mira imagined lying on a bed in carriage, slurping down apple au laits and gazing out the window at the passing countryside. "Reeeally nice... You've gotta hook me up with one of those."

"I promise you'll get a chance some other time."

"C'mon, Solomon, don't hold out on me. Why can't I take one to the catacombs?"

"The mission has to be kept top secret. Only one country uses the Pegasus Carriage and Caravan, and they're only used for state matters and transporting royalty. If you show up in one of those, there's going to be a lot of attention and a lot of questions."

"...Yeah, that would be inconvenient."

"Right? I'll set you up with a regular-looking carriage."

"Fine, I guess." Mira nodded and shoved another cookie into her mouth. But before she could swallow, the door to the office flew open and slammed into a nearby bookcase. Startled, Mira choked on the half-chewed pastry.

"Mission complete!" Luminaria struck a victorious pose and her fiery red hair fluttered about her. Mira gulped down her cup of tea in between coughs and gasps, glaring at the Elder Sorceress.

"Very well done." Solomon waved a hand in a show of gratitude, then glanced back down at the map on his desk, looking at the remaining four locations where hordes had been reported. He hadn't received reports of completion for those battles, but it wasn't surprising that Mira and Luminaria finished first. He was still worried.

"Oh, you're already back?" Luminaria closed the door and turned to see Mira pouring another cup of tea while blinking tears from her eyes. "I thought I'd be the first."

"You were close. If you'd been an hour earlier, you'd have beaten me."

"Well, my target was an hour further away, sooo..." Luminaria sat on the edge of the office desk as though it were her usual perch. She looked at Mira with a curious eye, and asked, "What do you think of the FAV?"

"I'm telling you—that thing is in dire need of seat belts," she said, taking another sip of tea. "And Garrett drives like a madman."

Luminaria shifted her gaze to Solomon, narrowing her eyes. "See! I told you we needed seat belts!"

"Point taken. I'll consider it." Solomon nodded reluctantly and then pulled a camouflage helmet from a drawer of his desk. "But I still think a tanker helmet has a certain flair to it.'"

He pulled on the helmet, looking sulky but proud. Then he took a piece of paper from the top of his desk before edging up close to Mira, like a child trying to get their parent to sign a permission slip.

"By the way, while we're on the subject, I was hoping you could make me a bunch of Refining Stones and Magic Stones. That will let us improve the operation of the FAV and run more experiments on the Accord Cannon while you're gone. I'll supply the materials, of course!"

The paper was filled with a detailed list of the types and

numbers of items needed. Solomon smiled expectantly and nodded. Sure, they'd be useful to his country, but they would also feed his personal interests.

"Hrmmm. There's a lot here. What rank of Magic Stones do you need?" Mira said, looking over the sheet. Solomon's smile grew even brighter.

"I'd like as high a rank as possible, but for the moment, I'll take quantity over quality. If you could make sure that at least five of each are rank three, that would be great."

Magic Stones were graded on a seven-point scale, with rank one the most powerful and rank seven the least. Input materials determined the final grade, and as such, rank-one Magic Stones were incredibly rare.

"All right, that's fine. But it would be faster if I did this back at the tower. I'm sure I have plenty of Refining Stones cluttering up one of my storerooms already. Probably some Refining Quartz, Refining Crystals, and Magic Stones as well."

"That makes sense. If you'd shown up sooner, I might already have my Type 10. We'd at least be a little further down the development chain. Still, I'm not going to look a gift horse in the mouth." Solomon sat back down with a contented grin; he loved it when a plan came together.

"If you needed them that bad, you could have just asked Mariana. She has access to all that stuff when I'm away—and she probably has a better idea of where they are than I do." Mira suspected the fairy had been shuffling things around for three decades for lack of anything better to do.

"Heh...about that. I tried asking her if you had any Refining Stones or Magic Stones in your storeroom once, and if I could have some," Solomon said with a bitter chuckle.

"Did you now? Did you use them all, then?"

"Mmmm...no. She wouldn't have any of it. Absolutely refused to part with any of your belongings, even to me. She said you'd be coming back and that it was her mission to protect the tower so that you wouldn't be inconvenienced when you returned...and then she started crying."

"Oh, yeah," chimed in Luminaria. "I was there with him. She looked ready to defend that tower with her life."

"I see..." said Mira. *Even if my new look is a state secret, I should at least tell Mariana the truth.*

Her mind pictured a sad, lonely girl with beautiful sapphire hair. And the only person who could make her happy again was Mira. Leaving her in tears was a far cry from the ideal man that Mira aspired to be. Mira resolved to tell her the truth the next time they met—that she was Danblf.

...And then she realized she couldn't do it. Not out of cowardice or shame, but because the situation in the kingdom demanded absolute secrecy. The truth had to wait until the other Wise Men were located and restored to their towers.

"I'll leave what's in your storeroom to your discretion." Solomon continued, oblivious to Mira's inner struggle. "But for now, what's on that list will do nicely. I'll show you where the palace refining room is later."

"Hrmmm, then I'll see what I can get done before bed tonight."

"The palace refiners would have a fit if they heard you say that," Luminaria said with a smile from her position on the desk.

They worked away day and night to supply materials for the research effort. If they saw Mira speed through her refining task in a couple of hours, they might never recover from the damage to their morale.

"We'll have a refining station and materials moved to your bedroom." Solomon said after a moment, realizing that outcome was likelier than he would care to admit. "If you could do the refining in secret, that would be for the best."

"No sweat," said Mira, placing her teacup on the table. "But on that topic, wouldn't it be better if you could be self-sufficient?"

"Well...yeah. But it takes study time and practice materials to get better at the techniques. They're barely keeping up with production requirements as it is. Do you have any tips?" Solomon looked at Mira with hopeful eyes.

"Maybe. Depends on how good they are. Do you have paper and a pen I could borrow?"

"Sure, uh, here you are." Solomon took a fountain pen from his desk and a piece of parchment from a shelf and handed them to Mira.

"Gimme a minute." Mira spread the parchment on the table and began filling it with symbols and letters. "There we go, something like that. Go ahead and show this to your refiners later."

Luminaria snatched the parchment from Mira and frowned as she squinted at all the shapes and symbols. Quickly giving up, she passed it over to Solomon. "This just looks like gibberish to me."

"This...huh, okay. I can tell it has something to do with refining. You think they'll understand this?"

"Yep."

The shapes and symbols were the plans for a new refining station that she'd been researching and devising in her spare time. In her spare time thirty years ago, more like, but better late than never. The diagram should be understandable to anyone who practiced refining as a living, but she made a point to scribble extra notes and details in the margins to make sure. Little did she know that she'd just handed over the key to a major breakthrough in technomancy.

"Back to the manhunt." Solomon said, removing his tanker helmet and putting it back in his desk. "I'll arrange for a carriage, and you should be able to leave for the catacombs first thing in the morning."

"Eh. No need to rush. I wouldn't mind a few days to relax before leaving." Mira illustrated her point by stretching out on the sofa as far as she could reach; every last inch of her body was exhausted.

"Really? I mean, if that's what you want. I was only trying to look out for you. Keep your best interests at heart and all that."

"My best interests?" Mira turned a suspicious gaze on Solomon.

"Yep. Look, it'll make the maids really happy if you decide to stick around for a few days," he said with a shrug.

"What are you talking about?"

"Just being a king, you know...I hear things. The head maid was telling me earlier today about how happy the staff was to have a young lady around. The outfit you were wearing when you arrived really inspired them—they've had so many ideas for pretty dresses over the years with no one to wear them. So many cosmetics have gone unused."

Luminaria snickered and added, "Aren't you lucky?"

"I leave with the dawn."

"Heh. Understood. I'll make the arrangements."

Mira didn't want to know what plans the servants were making for her, and she wasn't going to stick around to find out. They found the improvised magical-girl getup...inspiring? She shuddered.

"What did they see in that thing...?" she said before popping to her feet. "Where's your toilet?"

"Just through that door." Solomon pointed to a small door in the corner of the office.

"Thanks." With that, she quickly opened the door and ducked inside to take a look around. "Of course, a king would have a toilet that would rent for 100,000 yen a month."

A few moments later, Mira returned from the washroom feeling refreshed. She was immediately captured in a headlock by a brightly smiling Luminaria.

"Well, then, why don't we head to the million-yen baths?" Tucking Mira under her arm, she dragged her off to the changing room.

After washing up, Mira enjoyed a dinner with Solomon and Luminaria before the three retired once more to Solomon's office. Solomon slipped into a lecture on military strategy, and Mira yawned softly.

"Oh, is it already that late?" Luminaria checked the time and saw that it was almost midnight. "That came quickly."

"Why don't we call it a night? We can continue this later." Mira drank the last of her apple au lait and stretched out as far as she could.

"Ah, sure, sounds like a plan," said Solomon.

Mira nodded, hoping that he'd forget about the military lecture by then.

"Your room is the same as yesterday. Do you remember where it is?"

"Yeah, I'll manage." Mira got up and made her way to the door, nonchalantly leaving her empty bottle behind on the sofa. "G'night."

"You have an early start tomorrow, so don't wear yourself out with any funny business," said Luminaria with a leer.

"I won't do anything you would do."

21

Eyes still half-closed, Mira wandered into the bathroom to take care of business as the sun rose.

A few minutes later, she stumbled back into the bedroom and collapsed into bed, where her hand brushed up against an unknown object.

"What the...?"

Grabbing whatever she'd accidentally touched, she tried to fling it away. But as her eyes cracked open, she noticed the bunny ears popping out between her fingers. A piece of paper slipped from the anomalous item and floated down to the bedsheets.

It read:

We've taken the liberty of preparing you suitable sleeping attire. We hope you enjoy it.

Sincerely,

The Maid Staff

A cold chill ran down Mira's spine.

Currently, she was just wearing her skivvies, and these pajamas were the reason. She'd returned to her room last night to find a full-on bunny onesie neatly folded by her pillow. Naturally, Mira wanted nothing to do with it.

War had been declared on her fashion sensibilities, and this was the opening volley. Only heartache and strife lay ahead, and the palace was shaping up to be the front line.

Mira quickly pulled up her in-game menu to check the current time: 8:45 in the morning, well past time to get out of town. She began planning her retreat, mulling over the best way to get to the carriage garage without being noticed.

Planning was swiftly interrupted by a soft knock on her bedroom door.

"Good morning, Miss Mira. I've prepared you an outfit for today." The voice calling from the other side of the door was feminine and excited.

Oh, no! She's got the clothes with her! Mira cringed as the thought of whatever new fashion atrocity was about to be thrust upon her.

She cast her gaze about her room in a panic, but her only options were the bunny pajamas and the blue dress from the day before. She was desperate. Surely there had to be some way out of this?! Trapped in indecision, her time ran out.

"No response. Perhaps she's still in bed? Well, that won't do; her breakfast is getting cold. I'll just have to wake her up," said the maid flatly, as if reading from a script. Then the door opened.

The maid entered the room, and the first thing she saw was Mira's petite bum and legs hanging over the edge of the bed.

Completely lost in panic. Mira had shoved her head under the covers to hide. If she couldn't see them, perhaps they couldn't see her. No such luck.

"Good morning, Miss Mira!" the maid chirped as she stepped over to the bed and pulled back the opulent duvet.

"Morning."

"My name is Lily, Miss Mira, and I've been assigned as your personal maidservant. I promise to do my very best."

"Th-thanks..." Mira's shame gave way to agony when she saw the outfit in Lily's hands.

It was the epitome of gothic lolita, a black-and-white affront to good taste. The dress featured a white sleeveless top paired with a flared black skirt, topped with a robe that looked like an open-fronted fitted coat. The whole ensemble was festooned with frills, ribbons, and lace wherever possible.

Her protestations were ignored and she was transformed yet again into Magical Girl Mira, much to her chagrin.

The only request Lily granted was Mira's demand to forgo the intricate lace-trimmed drawers. She stuck to the relatively plain panties with the single small bow on the front.

After she was dressed, Mira was escorted to a room in the maids' quarters—the only room in the palace forbidden to men. It seemed like the entire maid staff was crammed in to witness the spectacle.

Lily wrapped a measuring tape under her arms and around her bust, ensuring that they tailored her bra in the correct size. The ladies knew that panties might have a little stretch to them, but an ill-fitting bra would be a special kind of hell.

As Lily insisted that this was a necessity, Mira muttered, "Just do as you please…"

"All right, Miss Mira, hands up!" Lily commanded. Mira complied like a dull-eyed puppet.

In fairness, Mira hadn't done much heavy exercise, but she had noticed that her clothes chaffed in certain delicate places. She conceded the point…silently.

"You're so cute! I'm jealous."

"Is that so…" murmured Mira sullenly.

How long will this torture last…?

After taking a few more measurements, Lily moved around behind Mira. Then she reached forward and gently cupped Mira's twins to ascertain her cup size. The particulars of her bust confirmed, Lily sent the information off. Another maid rushed in with a perfectly fitted bra a few minutes later.

"How's that, Miss Mira? Does it hurt or make it hard to breathe?"

"No. But it feels strange."

"That's perfectly normal for your first bra," said Lily with a warm smile.

Despite the maids' gentleness, Mira let out a grand sigh at the sight of herself. She never would have guessed that being doted on could feel so oppressive. While it may have seemed that they were just having fun at her expense, she grudgingly recognized their professionalism. The workmanship of the garments and their attention to detail were impeccable.

"Thank you for your patience, Miss Mira. Once you return, we'll have many costu...er, *outfits* made with your proper measurements in mind," Lily said while helping her back into her robe.

Solomon wasn't the only person in the palace with a secret weapons program.

After being introduced to the rest of the maids, Mira was led back to the dining hall for breakfast; bread, soup, salad, and fruit juice helped her perk back up. She had to admit that the outfit suited her—an observation that she would keep to herself, fearing future wardrobe improvisation by the staff.

As she finished her juice, Mira looked up and noticed that she'd become the center of attention.

Why are they staring at me?

She shrunk in her seat, looking nervously around the room at the other guests who were now looking back at her. She tried to hide in her robe to avoid the stares.

That anxious behavior ignited Lily's maternal instinct, and the maid rushed to Mira's side. Gently coaxing her from her chair, she hustled Mira out of a side door while casting withering glares at anyone who had the gall to continue staring at the small lady.

After making their escape, Lily soothed Mira as she escorted her to the king's office.

"My king, I have brought Miss Mira." Lily knocked at the door and announced her presence.

"Very well, come in," came Solomon's voice.

Lily opened the door and bowed. After Mira entered the office, she gently closed the door and waited outside the room.

"Well now, good morning."

"Yeah, g'morning." Mira returned the greeting and then flopped exhaustedly on the sofa.

As Solomon got a good look at her outfit, he covered his mouth with a hand as his shoulders shook. Mira turned and glared at the eternal boy-king.

"Did you sleep well?" he asked.

"Too well. I missed my chance to escape the maids."

Solomon could no longer contain his laughter. "It suits you! As always, the maid staff delivers."

"I just wanted an ordinary robe." Mira fingered the ruffle on the edge of her skirt with a wry smile. It was hard to believe that the dress had been made in just a day or two.

"By the way, thanks for getting that refining work handled."

"Sure. The Magic Stones are kicking around my room somewhere." said Mira. "I didn't have time to get them into my inventory before my dress-up session started this morning."

"They were already collected by the staff. That should fuel our experiments for a little while. Thank you."

"Don't mention it," Mira replied, waving off the thanks. Then she settled back against the sofa, still getting used to the unfamiliar feeling around her chest.

"Ah, yes, before I forget. I wanted to give you this." Solomon tossed a bag to Mira. A clinking metallic sound came from inside.

"Hrmmm? What's this?" Mira asked as she shook the bag and listened to the jingling.

"Money. Funds for your trip."

"Why are you giving me this? I've got plenty of cash."

"Oh, really? Is it stored in your tower storeroom?"

"What are you talking about? It's here in my..." She tried to pull 100 ducats from her inventory, but nothing happened.

"How's that working out for you?" Solomon smiled mischievously.

Mira hurriedly pulled up her status screen to check her cash total. She stared in horror.

"Wh-where's all of my money?!"

"It vanished in a puff of electrons when this world became real, probably. The prevailing theory is that since it was just a number on a spreadsheet, there was no logical way for it to make the transition. It all just disappeared."

"I had a quarter-billion ducats..." Mira collapsed on the sofa and buried her face in her hands.

"Dang... Well, now you know how I felt."

They spent a few moments in silence, mourning in solidarity.

"So anyways, you need physical money now. Consider it a reward for your actions yesterday. That should be enough to get by on until you come up with a side hustle. That always was your specialty."

The bag held just a few coins. One gold coin, three mithril, three silver, four cobalt, and ten copper. The gold coin counted as 50,000 ducats, the mithril were 10,000 each, the silver 5,000, the cobalt 1,000, and the copper was worth 100.

"One hundred thousand... Just one hundred thousand...?"

"Come on, cheer up. You'll make it all back." His words were soothing, but his tone certainly wasn't. Then he perked up with an impish twinkle in his eye. "Actually, that reminds me of another issue. Have you used your Item Box since you've returned?"

"Yeah, a few times. What about it?" she asked sullenly.

"Doesn't seem like you've noticed yet."

Solomon took a fountain pen from his desk and tossed it over to Mira. She traced the arc of its flight and caught it before holding it up at eye level. From the look of it, it was just an ordinary fountain pen. An incredibly fancy fountain pen from a king's desk, but still a fountain pen.

"And?"

"Try putting it in your Item Box."

She wondered what he was getting at. She called up her Item Box and tried to store the pen, but it just fell to the ground instead.

"...Seriously?"

Mira watched the pen roll across the floor through the translucent window of her Item Box. She had plenty of inventory space available, so that wasn't the problem. She turned back to Solomon. He stood and picked up the fountain pen before opening his Item Box.

"More weirdness stemming from how the game categorized items. Pens and quills were categorized as miscellaneous items, while swords and armor and such were equipment items, and jewels and metals were material items, right?" As he spoke, he pulled out a sword from his Item Box.

"Soon after the game became reality, a few players banded together and created a research facility to determine the new laws of physics in this world. One of the things they discovered was that items had been automatically assigned to those tags by the game system. And, as the name implies, the Item Box can only store things that have been classified as *items*."

Solomon moved and took a book from a shelf, holding it up for Mira to see.

"But now that this is reality, the system is no longer assigning metadata tags to anything. This pen isn't a miscellaneous *item*, and this book isn't a document *item*. They're just a book and a pen, so they can't be stored in the *Item Box*. Luckily, whatever is already in your Item Box is already tagged so you won't have any issues there."

Solomon put the sword back into his Item Box.

"Well, that sounds like a pain. So, no more traveling light?" Mira lamented what she'd just heard. This would complicate logistics on her upcoming journey to find their fugitive Wise Men.

"But, about six months after the change, we devised a revolutionary work-around."

"Oh ho. Tell me more." Mira shot Solomon a pointed look, urging him to drop the theatrics and to speed up.

"They came up with a way to manually do what the system did automatically. A new skill, called Ethereal Art: Itemization. When it's used on an item, it applies the magical equivalent of a metadata tag and allows the item to be stored in an Item Box."

"So basically, with that technique, I can keep carrying all my stuff?"

"Bingo. And it's easy to use. Here, I'll teach you."

Solomon pulled a document from a bookshelf and spread it over the table before Mira. It contained detailed instructions on how to use the technique. She immediately set about learning it.

Thirty minutes later, Mira had mastered the technique without issue. She used it on the fountain pen and stored it in her Item Box. Success confirmed, she gave a satisfied nod and returned to the sofa with a sigh.

"One last thing, about the catacombs. Unlike the past, all dungeons are now managed by the Adventurers' Guild Union." Solomon said, turning the conversation back to Mira's upcoming mission.

"Guild Union? What's that?" Mira asked as she pulled out a few things that she'd put in her Item Box.

"It's an organization that was created after the change to prevent civilians and weak players from accidentally entering dungeons and dying."

"Ho ho... That makes sense. But doesn't that let them monopolize treasures from the dungeons?"

"They're on the level. There was an incident a while back... A kid wound up dying."

"Hrmmm, I see..." Mira was intrigued by Solomon's slight drop in tone.

He explained. Dungeons were home to hidden treasures, but they were also dangerous places overrun by monsters and beasts that were far stronger than those found on the surface. The temptation to seek riches had convinced many hapless people to delve deep into the darkness, never to see the light of day again. That much Mira already knew.

Back when this was a game, it was no big deal, but now the consequences for foolish actions were far more acute.

A child wandered into a dungeon. Their mother was ill, and they were in searching for flowers to make a special medicine. But as night fell, the child didn't return, and the adults all went in search. Just past the entrance of the dungeon, they found the body of the child, half-eaten and barely recognizable. The kid's hand was still clutching one of the flowers. When the mother heard the news, she passed away soon thereafter, as if following her child into the beyond.

This wasn't just flavor text in a game anymore. NPCs were real people now. They inhabited the world and their deaths left real sadness in their wake. A player heard about the incident and swore to never let such tragedy happen again. That was the birth of the Adventurers' Guild Union.

Requests flooded in. *I want to go exploring* and *I need specific materials only available in such-and-such dungeons.* So the organization began to manage the dungeons and serve as a mediator, granting requests and licenses to those who were capable.

Gradually, the organization grew to an enormous size and was permitted to establish branches in various countries, under the conditions that they wouldn't interfere with political disputes and they *would* assist with defense against attacking monsters.

"Anyway, naturally, you'll be a part of the Mages' Guild. I have a letter of recommendation for you." Solomon walked over to Mira with an envelope in hand, offering it to her with a smile.

"Huh, so this will get me in the dungeon?" After glancing at the front and back of the envelope, Mira quickly Itemized it as a document item and added it to her inventory.

"No. That will get you into the guild, and the guild gets you into the union. Only adventurers who belong to the union are allowed to enter the dungeons. The dungeons are given a rank that corresponds to difficulty. I believe the catacombs are a C-Rank dungeon. Your adventurer rank goes up as you complete quests for the union and they start to recognize your abilities. Unimaginative? Perhaps. But everyone understands how the system works and it gets the job done."

"Fair enough. So, as I rank up, I can take on more difficult requests. I've always liked that system." Hearing that a few game-like elements had survived the change made Mira slightly excited.

"The letter I gave you serves as a guarantee of your identity and competence. Usually, new registrants have to start at G-Rank, but that should bump you right up to C-Rank. Even a king doesn't have that much pull with union management."

"I see. Well, this should do." Having finished organizing her Item Box, Mira left the small items she'd practiced with on the edge of the table.

"Also, the union has two different branches, the Soldiers' Union and the Mages' Union. You can guess who belongs to each by the names."

"Hrmmm. Does the union have a presence here in Lunatic Lake? I might as well get this registration over with."

"They do. They're in most major cities. There's also one in the city near the catacombs. Are you sure you want to do it here? The wait time after application can take a full day." The way he was smiling implied something more.

"So, what? That just means I'd have to spend another night..."

Mira felt a sense of unease. The maids. She couldn't even imagine what sort of horror they would devise if given an entire day to prepare.

Mira faced a critical decision.

She could spend the night at one of Lunatic Lake's inns. But that came with the chance that she'd be captured when she returned to the palace the next morning to catch her ride to the catacombs. Alternatively, she could have the carriage come pick her up, but an overly enthusiastic maid might volunteer to tag along. Also no good.

No. Time was of the essence.

"Prep the carriage as soon as possible, please."

"Splendid idea! It's already done. You can leave whenever you like."

Mira jumped to her feet and followed Solomon out of the office.

Accompanied by Lily, Mira and Solomon made their way to the palace stables. There they found two horses and a coach a little larger than the Pegasus Carriage. Waiting alongside was another maid with a large basket and a garment bag in her hands.

"We somehow keep running into each other," Garrett said. He would evidently be serving as her driver.

Mira's expression tightened as she wondered how many bruises she'd gather today.

"Good morning, Miss Mira! It may not be the FAV or the Pegasus, but this carriage is still exceptionally fine! It is my honor to serve you again." Garrett bowed and, with a blissful smile, held out his hands as though introducing the seemingly ordinary carriage.

"I don't care about the carriage. I'm just begging you—please drive safely."

Garrett smiled and replied, "Of course!"

"Now then, take care," said Solomon.

"You too."

After exchanging farewells and being hugged tightly by Lily, Mira climbed into the carriage.

The other maid loaded up the basket and bag she'd been carrying. "Please do take care of yourself, Miss Mira," she admonished. "The basket contains food for your journey, and the bag has a change of clothes for you."

"I...I see. Thanks."

The maid bowed and then stepped away. Mira sighed in exasperation as she stared at the bag. She couldn't imagine...or rather, she didn't want to imagine what might be inside.

As the carriage gently pulled away, Mira felt a sense of relief and took a sip of apple au lait.

The scenery outside the window rolled past. She marveled at how the city had changed in three decades. Enjoying the sweetness of her drink, she watched the unfamiliar buildings go by.

After seeing Mira off, Solomon moved swiftly.

By hiding themselves in hordes of invading monsters, the Lesser Demons had exhibited a unique and troubling pattern of behavior.

He knew their targets: the flower fields with the white pillars. These were locations where the Angel Drop herb could be harvested, but there was nothing else that made those locations special, at least that he knew of. Now Solomon was worried he'd missed something important. Perhaps something more was hidden there. He decided to form a research team to assemble all the information they could find on Lesser Demons and the flower gardens.

Sending off instructions to have it done, Solomon looked out his window in the direction Mira's carriage had gone, and smiled.

CREATOR PROFILES

RYUSEN HIROTSUGU

Still suffering from childhood delusions. A fairy doctor said the case is terminal and there's nothing that can be done. Nevertheless, he isn't pessimistic and lives each day to the fullest. Even if he vanishes, he just hopes that he'll be remembered.

FUZICHOCO

An illustrator who was born in Chiba and now lives in Tokyo. Draws all sorts of things, but primarily works on books and card games. Lives on chocolate.